<u>Wingless Love</u>
By
Cheyenne Oconnor

For my wonderful husband who helped make this dream a reality and who inspired this story. I love you.

Sensitive content involving domestic violence, stalking, and murder.
Please mind your mental health as it matters greatly.
Domestic violence hotline: 800-799-7233 or text 88788

Ch.1

With an iced coffee in my hand, I sat on a bench at the edge of Samson's Park. I was looking over the many visitors that frequented on a warm September afternoon. With heightened telepathy, I tried to stay away from parks or any large crowd for that matter. One of the two people who knew my secret, FBI Special Agent Julia Kniles, called and begged for my help. I couldn't really tell my own sister no, no matter what it was. With her superiors breathing down her neck to find Seattle's own serial killer, I jumped at the chance to help her.

I sipped at my coffee again but couldn't take another as a woman jogged by. Her thoughts were arrogant but shaken at encountering someone she perceived to be a creep lurking on the trail. As I stood up, I looked at the van, knowing Julia was watching. I made my way in the direction the jogging woman had just come from. The homeless man on the bench was startled and his thoughts were panicked as I walked up to him, Julia joined me casually at my side.

I didn't mean to scare her, but that man was following her and he...

His eyes were wide with fear and hopelessness as he stared between Julia and me. Julia knew I had heard something from the look on his face.

"What is it?"

"He saw a man following a jogging woman. It probably wouldn't hurt to get him with a sketch artist. May be nothing, but..."

"Every little bit helps."

She waved to her crew, and they escorted the man to the van. I followed behind, ready to be done with the crowds and constant chatter. I stopped to throw my empty cup away and felt the hair on my neck stand. I scanned the park quickly and found a man that now seemed to stick out in the crowd. He was standing at the far side of the fountain. One word sang through his mind as he watched me: *Mine.*

At my modest three-bedroom apartment that night, I trembled slightly still feeling that man's eyes lingering on my skin. When I closed my eyes, I could still see him. Tall, muscular, and he oozed with malevolence.

Sleep proved to be fruitless. I retreated to my bathroom where I cherished my antique, claw-footed, porcelain tub. Julia said it was a waste of money to have it installed in my apartment, but it was my sanctuary. I sank beneath the steaming water and attempted to relax. A flash of an image had me bolting upright, causing water to splash over the rim. He was in my head. Not like before. Not like a memory, but actually in my head. He spoke in an ancient language that matched his gruff voice. I wrapped in a towel and went straight for my computer. I typed in the words as best as I could remember. I was astonished. The language he spoke was Aramaic. He whispered in my head: *My Angel*.

I needed answers. There was only one person who could call. Jethro's theory about us being fallen angels was ludicrous. Even Julia said so. Now, I wasn't so sure. I looked at the clock on my phone. 3:28 a.m. I took a deep breath and dialed his number. He answered on the second ring.

"Good morning, Selena. It's a bit early for you. Everything alright?"

"I need you."

I didn't even recognize my own voice as it came out in a panicked whisper. Everything came pouring out after that. How terrified had I actually been?

Ch.2

I saw her. After centuries on this earth, I finally found her. She spun around and those mahogany curls flew over her shoulder. Her deep fawn brown eyes locked onto mine and my heart stopped. Something wasn't right, though. Those eyes held no recognition. My angel didn't know me. Was this my punishment? To find her once again, but for her to have no memory of me? That revulsion added fire to the demon furor that had originally landed me on the FBI's most wanted list. I've killed multitudes of women in the hunt for my angel. I was disappointed, however, to discover that my beautiful angel appeared to be working with the agent on my case. I wanted that one dead more than anyone else. Sadly, if my angel was close to the agent, I wouldn't touch her. I couldn't risk hurting my angel. I ached inside from her lost and broken look, and I yearned to wrap my arms around her. I had to find her. Let her know she wasn't alone anymore. I pondered on the how. Then, it hit me; the agent.

I searched the FBI database. Special Agent Julia Kniles. I clicked on her profile and scanned through her information.

-Top of her class at the academy

-Excellent marksmanship

-Dedicated to the job

-Transferred from Quantico to Seattle to be with her only living relative; her sister.

-Parents died in a robbery gone wrong. She and her sister were out when it happened.

I looked up the reports and other news that I could find related to the robbery. I saw her picture. My angel. Her name is Selena. I tried to read on, trying not to just stare at the picture on the screen. The robbery had motivated Julia into the law enforcement field. Selena, on the other hand, went into psychiatry. She was Seattle's top therapist. Also, she has awards for being world renowned in therapeutics. Angel is telepathic. The profession suited her. With such an obvious sign, I had renewed hopes that I could get her to remember me. I walked to the window, staring at the vast city I had made my hunting grounds. With her picture still on the screen, I closed my eyes to see her with my mind's eye. I whispered to her from my heart, willing her to hear me. I felt a pang in my chest as I realized whether or not my angel would even accept me after all the murders I had committed.

I had to get out of my head. She was here, but not yet mine. I felt the vehemence boiling inside. My fist made contact with the drywall, leaving a gaping hole. The only way to get close to angel was through the sister. I was determined. I left my apartment intent on killing again. I walked the back alleyways looking for fresh prey. The night was cool and clear. I saw a woman rush from the back entrance of a restaurant to her car. Paranoid. I smiled at my luck. This was an immaculate situation. I rushed her, hitting her from behind. She didn't even have time to scream as she crumbled effortlessly to the pavement. I carried her limp corpse to her trunk. Blood trialed us around the car. I found myself irritated instead of relieved. I stood displeased at the realization that no kill would have the same satisfaction. I already found my angel. No female kill would be that pleasurable again. I needed something more. Something different. More of a challenge. I heard the back door squeal open. I looked over and saw a man step into the night for a cigarette. I stood perplexed for a moment as I thought it through. I walked up to him, appearing like a friendly bystander.

"Hey, man. This lady needs help. Says she can't get her car to start."

The man grinned as he shook his head, not surprised by my words.

"Sally. I told her to wait for me."

I followed him as he walked past me. He knew the danger he was in too late after seeing the blood trail. I snatched him around the neck. He struggled ineffectively to get free. With a jerk of my arm, his neck snapped. He tumbled to the pavement just as she had. I felt the brief euphoric rush and smiled, satisfied.

At home once more, I felt confident. I switched on the TV. It was always tuned into the local news. I turned up the volume before heading to my shower. Afterwards, I stood naked at my window with my second glass of bourbon. A sinister smile stretched across my face as the sirens wailed through the city. I was confident these murders would make the morning news.

I could only think about her. My beautiful angel. I was determined that I would make her remember me. I would die trying if I had to. Then again, I can't be killed so I can't fail.

Ch.3

Jethro wasted no time. When he knocked, I was still flustered, but relief filled me. He hugged me and went to the kitchen. I sat down at the island while he fixed us cups of coffee.

"Are you sure that's what he said?"

"Yes! I even looked it up!"

"Who is this guy?"

Jethro began to pace the floor, his anger rising steadily.

"I have no idea."

"He got into your head, Selena!"

"I know that Jethro! Why do you think I called you."

I hadn't realized I started to shake until Jethro came over and took the coffee from my hand. He let out a defeated sigh and wrapped me in his arms. Suddenly, he raised an eyebrow at me. We were both noticing my state of dress, or more like undress. In my panic, I had only thought to put on a pair of panties and a t-shirt before Jethro knocked.

"Well, I certainly feel over dressed, now."

I laughed as he took me by the hand and led us to my bedroom. I sat on the edge of my bed as he joined my state of undress. I scooted back to the pillows as I couldn't help but stare at him. He stripped off his shirt, revealing biceps, pecks, and washboard abs. After his jeans were gone, I stared helplessly. He was mouth-watering. He caught my stare and smiled cockily before climbing in beside me. He put an arm around me and switched on the TV before kissing the top of my head.

"Offer still stands, you know, if you want to see what the rest looks like."

I smiled and snuggled into him, content.

"Maybe another time. I feel better already, just like this."

He pulled me a little closer to him and I laid my head on his chest. I hadn't noticed that I drifted off to sleep until I felt Jethro tense and start to get up at a knock at my door. Before I could tell him it was just Julia, she was the only one with a spare key to my apartment, she walked in. She stopped dead with a violent blush creeping up her neck and staining her face when she turned around.

"Well, this is a pleasant surprise."

"I'm sure you think so, Jules."

I climbed out of bed with Jethro. He pulled on his jeans and went to grab for his shirt. I grabbed it from him with a playful smirk as I held it up to my nose and breathed in his scent. He smiled with a shake of his head as he went to my closet and grabbed one of his sweatshirts. He kissed my cheek and left without a word to Julia.

After hearing the door click closed, she turned to me with a teasing smile. I just rolled my eyes at her. Jethro was a world-renowned fighter. In the ring, it was like he knew what you were going to do before you did. He was unbeatable. An archangel is what he called himself, only to me. Julia thought I was being foolish by not tying him down. We went to the living room after I fixed two more cups of coffee.

"Now, what is so important that you had to come at 5:30 in the morning?"

Julia's face got really stern and serious. It had to do with the case.

"He's killed again. Something in him has changed, though. There were two victims. A woman and a man."

Something in her face changed as she spoke, and it worried me. What was it she didn't want to tell me?

"What is it?"

"You know one of our victims."

Ch.4

I stared at my TV as the six o'clock news broke about the murders. I watched as they were live at the scene. Perfect. I saw Special Agent Kniles in the background. With her, my angel stood out. Anguish filled me as I saw her distress. They pulled back the sheet on the guy I had killed, and I saw her gasp of horror followed by her tears. Had I killed someone my angel knew? Anger quickly took over as I watched. A man was there, not a cop or an agent. Someone that seemed too familiar with my angel. He led her away, off the camera view and I couldn't see her anymore. Imprudently, I went to the crime scene. People were everywhere. The media, the police and FBI, bystanders, plus the local day-to-day traffic. It was constant chatter for normal hearing. I knew my angel wouldn't be here. Infuriated, I walked off and found myself on a trail in a park. As I walked, I saw a couple strolling hand in hand, happily lost in each other. It reminded me of my angel and this man, and I lost it. I had never killed in broad daylight, especially so close to an active crime scene, but I no longer cared. Killing was so facile and effortless to me. It was in fact my main specialty in Hell. After Lucifer dispatched me here, I felt the pull of my angel and knew I had to find her. Thousands of centuries ago, she was one of the purest things Heaven ever made, complete with white wings kissed by silver. Once upon a time, she astounded all, including myself, as she fell for me in a time of war. At that time, I was worth all the pain, loss, and heartache at her wings being stripped from her. It's what eventually killed her in the end and I thought I lost her. I speculated she'd be in Hell for it, but she was nowhere down there. I didn't know if the Father had decided to take her back or if he had forced her to wonder the earth like Brother Cain. None of that matter now. She was here and I had seen her. If I could get her to remember me, I know I would have her back in my arms. As I meandered the streets aimlessly, I began to challenge how she could even be here. I stopped abruptly as I saw her. She had walked into a building and without thinking, I followed her inside. I followed not close enough behind as she was gone from sight by the time I walked in. I went to the board in front of me and searched the names. Dr. Selena Kniles, 32nd floor. Impulse drove me to the elevator and I rode it up. When I got off, I was greeted by a young woman at the receptionist's desk.

"Can I help you?"

She seemed bright and cheery, but it was fake. She was holding some kind of pain back. I could tell from her eyes. I smiled at her professionalism.

"I was wondering about making an appointment."

"I'm so sorry, sir. At this time, Dr. Kniles isn't taking on any new clients. You could try back in a couple weeks if you'd like."

I knew I had hurt my angel. This man I killed was someone she knew. A client? A friend? Surely not a boyfriend. The man at the scene with seemed more likely to fit the description. I nodded my head in thanks before I left. My angel was right there. So close, I could taste her scent in the air. It wasn't time. I must be patient. I knew I would run into her again. Unfortunately, I knew I would end up killing again just thinking about this other man with her. I didn't want anyone touching my angel. She was mine and I was sure to make certain this man knew it before it was over with.

Ch.5

Julia drove me to the crime scene. I was unsure what to expect. She had said one of the victims was a client. She had remembered seeing him before but couldn't recall his name. Once we got there, they pulled back the sheet and I lost it. Laying on the ground with his neck snapped was a long-time client of mine: Thomas Stanly. He had severe childhood traumas after watching his father in a drunken rage shoot his mother and then killing himself. He was doing so well and making great progress. He even started talking to his sister again. That had been a major breakthrough as he couldn't have any contact with any of his family before. He didn't deserve this.

Julia saw my reaction and got on the phone with Jethro. She knew he'd be the only one to get me calmed down again. He showed up and wrapped an arm around my shoulder and led me away from the crime scene and all the people. The noise on top of everything had become unbearable. He took me for coffee. Hazelnut frappes. We walked for a bit down the sidewalk. I thanked him for helping me but told him I needed to go into the office. I had to collect Thomas' things for Julia to contact next of kin. His daughter was going to be devastated. He kissed my cheek and told me he was headed to the gym, but to call if I needed anything.

In the office, I went through the filing cabinets in the back room. My receptionist, Lydia, was a mess in her own head. Thomas was well known in here and he was a sweet guy. I think they even went out for a coffee once, but I was unsure. As I sorted and listened to her thoughts, I felt a wall go up in her head. She was in professional mode, which meant someone was here. A dark uneasiness filled the atmosphere of the office, and a chill ran through me as I heard those words again: *My Angel*. My hands began to shake as I switched on the security monitor in the room. It was the same man from the park. I heard him ask Lydia about making an appointment. I felt a weight lift as Lydia told him I wasn't seeing any new clients. I watched shocked and surprised as he simply nodded and left. I had Lydia's thoughts once more as he walked away: what a creep.

I was so flustered and fearful; all I wanted at that moment was Jethro. I called his cell, and it went to straight to voicemail. His phone was off. I called his gym and his receptionist, Angie, answered.

"Knight's Gym. How can I help you?"

"Hey, Angie, it's Selena."

"Of, Selena! We heard about Thomas. I am so sorry, sweetheart."

Angie was an older woman in her late forties and had been working for Jethro since he decided to open his own gym. She was sweet and motherly to everyone, and it felt nice at that moment.

"Thank you, Angie. It hasn't been easy, getting his files together. I tried Jethro's phone, and it went straight to voicemail. Everything okay?"

"Oh, yes. He's in the practice ring with a few new recruits. Shall I have him call you back once he's done?"

"No need. Just let him know I called, please."

"Sure thing, sweety. You take it easy, okay?"

"I will, thanks Angie."

With that, I hung up. I went to my office after stopping by Lydia telling her that she made a good call with not seeing new clients. I told her, in fact, I would probably shut the office down early today considering what happened. I sat in my office chair, thinking about how cruel the world had become. The stories I heard from my clients...nightmares wish they could be as scary. Now, I had one of my own. What did this guy want from me? I thought about calling Julia, but she had so much on her plate right now, I couldn't do that to her. I finally walked out, telling Lydia to close down the office for the day. On the sidewalk, the chatter was so immense. I closed my eyes to turn it all off. I couldn't deal with the flood of voices today. On top of it all, I could feel eyes on me. Maybe I'm just being paranoid. The silence was broken by the phone ringing. Jethro.

"Hey, Jet."

I didn't know my voice still shook and knowing Jethro, he could tell with the first letter that came out of my mouth.

"What's wrong?"

I told him what happened as best as I could without breaking down right there on the sidewalk in front of my own office building. The distress in his voice makes me think that maybe I'm not being paranoid as I think I am.

"Come to the gym. You'll stay at my place tonight."

I knew he was being serious. I was relieved, but I still tried to protest.

"Jet..."

"I'm not playing around. Have you told Julia?"

"No. Jules has enough to deal with, Jethro."

I heard that defeated sigh of his and knew he was giving up temporarily on not telling Julia.

"Fine. Just get here so I know you're okay. I mean it, Selena. Don't make me come find you."

"Alright, Jet. I'm hailing a cab now."

I hung up as the cab pulled up. I ducked inside, still feeling those eyes on me, but I dared not look around. I tell the driver where to head. At the gym, Angie greets me, and her heartfelt warmth forces me to smile as she hugs me. I walked back to Jethro's private office and slumped onto the couch. I propped my feet up and laid my head back. I'm not sure when or even for how long, but I ended up dozing off on his couch. I saw the man in my head again as I slept. He said the same thing to me: *My Angel.* This time, though, it was different. It was as if he were actually here. I smelt the stench of his breath and the warmth of it on my skin. I jolted upright, right into Jethro's protective embrace. He held me close and tried to sooth my shaking nerves from the experience. I was more terrified than I dared admit, but the more I shook, the closer and tighter Jethro held me. He had almost calmed me completely down when my phone rang, making me jump even more. Frustrated, Jethro took it from me. It was Julia.

"Hey, Julia, now's not a very good time........Well, it can wait.......I understand, and I don't give a damn.... Something has happened to your sister........Look, I'm not going to sit here and explain or argue with you on the phone. Just meet us at my place soon.... Because she's staying with me.... That's how bad it is.... Yeah, see you in a bit."

Jethro hung up and met my stare. He shook his head at my pleading look.

"Whoever this son of a bitch is, he terrifies you. You can deny it all you want, but I know better than that. She needs to at least know, Selena."

"She's been so busy with this case. I don't want to trouble her."

"And we don't know what this guy is capable of. If something were to happen to you...."

I could do nothing but put my head down and nod. He was right. Julia would be devastated and beside herself.

"Come on. I'm taking you home with me until further notice."

I smiled and nodded again. Jethro has always been over-protective of me. I didn't realize just how shaken up I still was until I went to get up and ended up sitting right back down. Jethro picked me up bridal style and walked out. Angie gasped when she saw me as she ran to open the door. Jethro told her I would be okay, but I had a stalker. In the parking lot, I could feel those eyes on me again. The uneasy feeling made me grip Jethro's neck a little tighter which made him tighten his grip on me. He set me down in the car and I closed my eyes and willed the feeling to just vanish.

We got to the parking garage of Jethro's condo building and I could walk on my own legs again. Granted with Jethro's assistance because he refused to let me go. The elevator went straight to Jethro's entryway. He had to have a code to get up there. Inside, I sat on the couch while he put his bag down and went to the kitchen. He came back with a mint green tea with honey for me. A jumped a bit at the knock on the door. Jethro opened it for Julia and she walked straight in. I smiled at seeing my overnight bag in her hands. She shrugged as she sat it down. She sat down across from me with a tight smile on her face.

"Jethro made it seem serious, so I thought you might need it."

"Thanks, Jules."

"Now, mind telling me what's going on? It's not the case is it? Because if it is, I can...."

"Jules, slow down. It's not the case."

"Then...."

Jethro had lost his patience for the day, especially with Julia.

"Selena has a stalker."

Ch.6

I watched as she walked out of the office building. She looked around and closed her eyes, trying to block out all the voices. She opened her eyes and pulled her phone out. Anger coursed through me at the smile that graced her face at whoever was calling. After a few minutes, she hailed a cab and hung up as she climbed inside. I walked down to my own car and followed her. She stopped in front of a gym. What was my perfect angel doing at a gym? I waited for her, thinking it was surely a mistake that she was here. Turns out, she was right where she wanted to be as she was in there for an hour or so. I kept willing her to hear me as I said her name over and over again. I became more intense as every minute went by without seeing her.

Finally, the doors opened and I perked up. Hot, boiling rage threatened to consume me as the same man from this morning now had her in his arms carrying her to a car. I watched as he put her in his car and drive off with my angel. I followed him. Where was he taking my angel? He pulled into a parking garage that went underground and didn't come back out. Half an hour later, I sat on the opposite side of the building when Agent Kniles pulled up. She had a bag in her hand. The rage burned even brighter inside me as I realized my angel was staying with this man. Why would angel do something like this to me? I got out, intent to storm in there and just take her. I stopped just in front of the entrance. What was I thinking? Angel didn't know me yet and Agent Kniles was up there. I shook my head. Angel was making me careless. Not good.

I walked to a small bar down the road and order a few beers. I should've known better. After my sixth beer, I still felt nothing but the burning rage inside me. I would need something stronger. A person, perhaps. After paying my tab, I walked back to my car in the pouring rain. I passed an alley where an elderly woman was trying to use a cardboard box to take shelter from the rain. Homeless. I walked down the stinking alleyway, right past her. She didn't even notice me. Before I reached the end, I walked back towards her. This time, she paid me attention, but too late. She went to scream as I covered her mouth and nose with my hand. She fought and struggled with me for her life as she shook from the lack of oxygen. I left out a moan as I feel the life slip away from her as I let her slide to the ground at my feet.

I walked back to my car with a smile on my face. I stopped at the condo building once more first. Agent Kniles' car is gone, but I know my angel is still in there. I shock myself at realizing why the old woman's kill had been so good; it's what I would've have done to my angel for her betrayal. I shook this off. Instead of going home, I go to this gym to see if I can figure out all I can about the man she was staying with. Was he just a member or was he the one that owned it, managed it? I would find out everything I could about Knight's Gym and all those who went there if I had to until I found this man my angel clearly trusted so much. I swore never to hurt my angel, but I would have to just this once. On purpose. I needed this man out of the way so I could get to my angel. But how to dispose of him?

"A stalker!"

Julia was livid. Almost like she took it as a personal offense someone would stalk me. Jethro was sitting next to me as Julia paced the floor.

"How sure are you?"

"I saw him that day at the park. That was the first time. Then, today, the same man was at my office."

I could see Julia processing everything I had just said. Her cop brain was working, now. Jethro added his own note to the situation.

"Selena shakes just thinking about this man. I don't like it."

Julia nodded her head and took a deep breath. She looked at me and I could tell she was no longer my sister, but Agent Kniles. She sat down in front of me and took a pad and pen out.

"I'll need to see your security footage from the office. Check and see if this guy gave us a good view of his face or not."

"Sure. You have a key to the office. Lydia has the rest of the day off anyway, so it should be empty."

"Okay. I also agree with Jethro. Stay here until we know it's safe for you to go back home. We don't know who this guy is or what he wants or even how much he knows about you. I'm also pulling you from the case. I don't want you out on the streets if I can help it. I'll bring more clothes if you need them."

I wanted to protest, but how could I? Julia and Jethro were not going to let me get hurt in any way. Julia hugged me before heading to the door. She warned Jethro to take good care of me and he just shook his head.

Once she was gone, Jethro took my bag into the bedroom. I shook my head at realizing how stupid I was. Here was this man that took such great care of me, been my friend for ages, and yet I always chose men like Elliot. Abusive knock-offs of the real thing. I closed my eyes and focused on his mind, his thoughts, but he felt my intrusion and responded.

I can feel you when you do that, you know.

"How?"

I hadn't realized I had asked out loud until I heard him walk to the bedroom door.

"I'm not sure. But you do know you don't have to poke around my head for anything. I'll tell you anything you want to know. Just ask me, Selena."

"Why are you doing all of this for me, Jethro?"

I turned and looked at him as I asked. He leaned a shoulder against the doorframe and crossed his arms over his chest with a serious look painted on his face and in that moment, he looked mouth-wateringly irresistible. His copper brown hair fell slightly over his forehead, but didn't meet his brow. He looked out the window as the rain began to fall and when his dark emerald gaze locked onto mine, I was taken aback by the change in their depths.

"I thought that much was obvious to you, doc."

He sounded tortured. He called me doc, which meant it was something I was supposed to notice, but didn't or refused to notice. I tried to defend myself while I thought it over.

"I know you care about me. You're my best friend. Plus, with the whole fallen angel thing...."

I was surprised by the stunned and hurt expression that crossed his face as he crossed the room to me and sat down next to me.

"Sure. But, Selena, it's so much more than that."

I was confused and I guess it showed on my face as he took my hand in his in an intimate gesture that seemed to make him slightly nervous. He took a deep breath before meeting my gaze once more.

"I'm in love with you, Selena."

Ch.8

I could do nothing but stare at him with my mouth gaped open. I wasn't exactly sure what I thought my answer would be, but I know it wasn't a confession like that. I took my hand from his and scooted back slightly. The pain that crossed his face made me feel guilty in the pit of stomach.

"Are you sure that's even allowed for us?"

Did I really just ask that? What was I doing?

"Right now, you and I are only human. But remember, In 1 Corinthians 13, the bible states so clearly if you do not have love, then you have nothing. So, why would it be banned for us to love one another."

I hate it when he makes sense. What was I supposed to do now? He even threw scripture at me.

"Jethro...I...."

"I know your past, Selena. Probably better than anyone. I'm just asking you to give me a chance. To give us a chance. You know I'd never hurt you."

I sat and thought for moment. I realized that he was right, but how do I trust someone again like that, even Jethro. I knew that's why I was hesitating. I cared deeply about Jethro and I knew he cared deeply for me. He would never do anything intentionally to hurt me. Especially not the way Elliot did. I closed my eyes. I figured as long as I was going to be staying here, why not give it a shot with Jethro? I took a deep breath and looked right into those deep green eyes again.

"Okay. I trust you, Jethro,"

His answer was a wide smile as he pulled me in close into his arms. One thing I knew for sure, was that this was my favorite place to be in the entire world. Something about being in his arms just felt right to me. I wrapped my arms around his neck, wanting to be even closer to him. He responded by pulling me onto his lap. Before I knew it, he was kissing me and touching me in all the right places. It was like his hands and lips knew the secrets of my skin to spark every one of my senses. I didn't want him to stop. I did a little encouraging by slipping one of my hands down to his waist. It must've been what he was waiting on because he lifted me up and took us to the bedroom. He eased me onto the sheets as if I weighed nothing to him. I was mesmerized as I laid there watching him undress. I had seen Jethro in nothing but his boxer briefs plenty of times before, but this...this was something entirely different. I was hyperaware of just how masculine Jethro really was. He had a firm jawline covered in his copper brown hair. He had bulging biceps that made me feel safe and secure whenever he held me. He had rock hard pecks that gave way to his incredible washboard abs that I could just run my hands over all day and never tire of him. He looked like a Roman or Greek statue carved by some kind of athletic God. I always knew he was deliciously handsome, but as I laid there staring, my mouth wasn't the only thing watering to have a taste of him. He could tell how I was looking at him and gave me one of those earth-shattering smiles that had me biting the corner of my lip. He came to the bed and slipped my jeans off with such skill, even with my legs still feeling the effects of his smile. he sat me up and pulled my shirt off, kissing every inch he exposed on the way leaving my flesh in a thin layer of gooseflesh. He stared down at my almost naked body with a new hunger and appreciation. He covered my body with his own and claimed my lips in a possessive and dominant kiss. His hand traveled south towards my panty line. As he ventured below the elastic waistband, his phone rang in the other room. I felt the vibration of his groan on my lips before he got up and grabbed it.

"Jethro Knight.... Mrs. Calloway......No, please, it's alright. What can I help you with?........Again......Classes start next week. You can fill out the papers then......Cops?..... It's that serious? Goodness.....No, I agree. Tell them to hang out along with yourself and Shane. I'm headed that way now......Yep. Bye-bye."

He turned me with an apologetic look. I just smiled at him. This was one of the reasons he opened the gym. To give trouble kids a place to go to where they can let out all that anger.

"I'm really sorry. I wouldn't go unless I had to."

"I know. It's okay. What's going on?"

"Shane Calloway. He's got a juvey record a mile long already and he's only fourteen. If he doesn't get into some kind of program, they are locking him up to do some serious time."

"Oh my. Why don't you suggest that part of his program be to see me at your discretion. No extra charge."

"You'd do that?"

"Of course. You care about these kids. I want to help in any way I can."

"Thank you, Selena. Are you going to be okay by yourself for a bit while I handle this?"

"Of course. No one knows I'm even here. Go."

He smiled as he bent down and kissed me. He grabbed his coat and keys after getting dressed and was out the door. I got up and engaged the lock before going to take a shower to see if I could relieve the pulsating bud that was now left between my legs. It wasn't going to be as satisfying as the real thing, but it was some relief.

Ch.9

After leaving the condo building, I drove back to the gym. I stared at it for some time wondering how I was going to find out who this man was. The sun was starting to disappear behind the city skyscrapers when it felt like a bomb went off in my chest. Something was not right. Something was wrong with my angel. Without thinking, I sped off for the condos. I wasn't sure what had just happened but I didn't like it. Before I was even halfway there, I knew what it was. There was a shift in my head and my heart telling me she wasn't entirely mine anymore. This Jethro had said or had done something to shift her mind and heart away from me. I could still tell, however, that he hadn't branded her. That would never happen. Even with that thought, the rage consumed me in an uncontrollable flame. How much was she going to betray me in a single day?

I sped off, needing to put as much distance as I possibly could between her and I. I wasn't paying any attention and had to brake suddenly, almost tearing up my car and crashing it into the Seattle Harbor. I got out and surveyed the warehouses that lined the docks. This part of the docks was mostly abandoned. I needed to be alone. Her betrayal stung worse than Hell Fire.

As I walked past the warehouses along the docks, I heard laughter and became enraged anew. I slithered around, not wanting to be noticed by whoever was here. I picked up a lead pipe along the way. As I came around to the group, I swung on the first guy, taking them all by surprise. As I looked down, I was disappointed in myself as blood ran like a steady stream from the man I hit. Now I was down to three play things. I dragged the other three to the edge of the platform they were standing on and tied them up. I was going to enjoy beating them to death. Since I was going to beat them to death, why not vent to these men on how unloyal my angel was being? I struck man number one in the knee and he let a howl of pain, making me smile.

"You know what, you have my angel to thank for this. She betrayed me real good tonight. I just can't believe she'd do something like this to me."

I hit guy number three in the shin making him scream like I broke something. I didn't.

"I mean, I suffer eternal damnation for her, scour the earth for her, getting rid of all the fakes that try to be her, but she chooses this gym guy over me?"

Guy number three receives another blow. This time to his ankle. This time, I do break it for good measure.

"I mean, when is it going to be enough for her to realize that I put in all this work just to be with her?"

Guy number three tries to beg, realizing what is now happening as his other two companions are passed out. I used the end of the pipe and connected solidly into his gut, making him gasp for air.

"I'm not finished yet! The more I think about it, the more this is not technically her fault."

Guy number two wakes up and starts screaming. I walk over to him and shatter his knees with a few swings.

"Hush now! I'm talking. I have done everything I know to do for her. Why hasn't she noticed me yet? Why doesn't she want to come home with me?"

Guy number three starts squirming again and I break all his ribs on the left side to make him be still. Guy number one has been awake this whole time and thinks he can be big and bold and brave.

"I don't blame her. You are a psychopath. Who would want someone like you?"

That was it. He pushed me over the edge. I lifted him straight up. My demon-black eyes stared right through him. I wrapped the chain around his pathetic mortal neck and watched him as his body jerked as he hung from the chains. His two friends followed suit, boring me with their whimpers and pleas. Thought I was amused by their useless struggles, making their necks break even faster, it still wasn't enough. My anger hadn't subsided. See what you do to me, Angel?

I drove off, unsure of my next destination. I finally had to pull over. I was at a run-down laundromat, alone. The sound of the washers and dryers humming did little to ease my burning. I was trying to think straight, to focus, to calm down. A car pulled up and a little old lady walked in with an empty clothes hamper. She didn't glance my way, just like the woman in the alley. She walked to one of the larger dryers that was off and started to remove clothes from it, dumping them into the hamper. I didn't even realize what I was doing before it was too late. I got up and started walking to her and she didn't even notice me until I was right behind her. I shoved her into the now half-empty dryer and locked the door. She banged helplessly as I just stared at her. She started to beg for her life. Why do they always feel the need to beg? Like it ever helped. I saw her turn as white as the sheets as I took coins out of my pocket and inserted them into the dryer. I gave her a sinister smile as I hit the button for max load. I heard her anguished cries as she tumbled in the machine. Once silence filled the little place, the glass was filled with her blood as she now appeared to fit effortlessly with the rest of her laundry. I turned and walked out. Why didn't I notice the security cameras that were right above me?

I felt slightly relieved, but not by much. I decided to just go back home. Nothing would be satisfying tonight. Five bodies and I felt no relief and it was all her fault. No. It wasn't really her fault, right? After all, my angel didn't know me. How could she know she was betraying me? Yes. That had to be it. My angel had never betrayed me in the past. Even stood against the archangel, Michael, who adored her so much. I needed to get this man out of the way, I could try to win my angel back. I couldn't have this man tricking and confusing my angel away from me. I walked inside my apartment and the TV was still turned onto the news. I went to the shower and let the hot water wash over me. The woman in the dryer would be the first to be noticed. The men at the docks might take a few days and may not even be considered my work. That was alright. I needed time. I needed to figure out who this man was. I just needed my angel to remain strong and not give herself to this other man. My angel's body was mine for the claiming and mine alone. I would not tolerate anyone else even thinking about branding her as their own.

Ch.10

I was sitting on the couch, tuned into the news with a towel still around my head. Julia knocked on the door again. I poured us both a drink. We would need it. She was here to tell me about what she had just found out.

"So, your security footage got a great look of this guy. Troubling thing is, we ran him through DVM and NCIS and found nothing."

"So, what happens now?"

"I suggest you stay with Jethro. You are safe here. Just until we've figured this out. I also have locals working on it. We will find out who this guy is, okay."

"Alright. I trust you will handle it. I have some news for you, too."

She shot an eyebrow up in surprise. I knew she was curious.

"Jethro told me he loved me. We are sort of dating now."

Her voice matched the enthusiasm on her face.

"Oh, my goodness! That's so amazing!"

"Don't get too carried away. We are just seeing how things work out right now."

"Oh, Selena. You can't possibly think that Jethro is anything like Elliot?"

I sighed heavily. I knew she would mention Elliot. She got him locked up and thinks that makes her the baddest of all and I owe her for saving my life. As if. Jethro was with me when I woke up, not her. Granted, it was because of that she transferred offices, but still.

"I'm not. I know Jethro would never hurt me like Elliot. I just can't help it. I'm cautious. Elliot was a great guy at first, too, remember?"

Julia patted my hand, understanding. I got that weird hero vibe from her again and sighed.

"I understand. But don't let it stop you from being happy."

Now, I was skeptical of her definition of happy.

"Like you and Nathan are so happy?"

It was her turn to be defensive, like she always did.

"Hey! We make it work, okay."

"I don't see how. Both of your jobs require too much of your time. Apart."

"That's not true. Sometimes our jobs have us in the same place at the same time."

I rolled my eyes at her, not believing a word she said.

"So, where does Nathan's contracting company have him at now, anyway?"

"Miami."

Her tone said she resented the fact that he was in bikini central without her.

"And you're not worried?"

I knew she was going to lie before she said a word. Image was everything to her.

"Never. I know I can trust Nathan."

I read into her thoughts, needing to know how she really felt about him being so far away.

Of course I'm worried. I haven't seen him in six months while he lives down in bikini model central.

I inwardly shook my head. I would never tell her that I heard that. Instead, I played it off as if I hadn't listened in.

"Wish I could be that secure with someone."

She gave me a knowing smile as she tilted her head.

"Who knows? With Jethro..."

"Too early for all that, alright."

"I know it. I'm just teasing you. I'd better head off, though. There was a murder down in the lower end. Not sure if it's our guy or not yet."

"What happened?"

"A little old lady was stuffed into a dryer."

"That's terrible."

"Tell me about it. Crime scene photos were gruesome. Luckily, there were security cameras. Getting the footage is another matter entirely which is why locals want our help. Tracking down the owners of these things can be almost impossible."

"Well, knowing you, you'll get it done."

"Yeah. I have to. Give Jethro my best."

"I will. Be safe."

With that, she was gone. Before I could even sit back down, my phone was going off. I thought it was Jethro, but I still had nothing from him.

Ch.11

Lydia was calling me from her personal cell.

"Hey, Selena, I'm sorry it's so late."

"It's not all that late, Lydia. What's going on?"

"Julia filled me in when I saw her at the office. Left some paperwork behind. I thought it best to just close the office and do online appointments for a while. If that's alright with you, of course."

"This is one of the reasons I hired you, Lydia. That sounds perfect."

"I'm so sorry, Selena. Had I known...."

"It's fine. I didn't even know until I talked to Jethro about it."

"You sure you're okay?"

"Yes. I'm doing just fine."

"Alright, well, Brain Dunaway called for you again. Says it's an emergency."

"I'm grabbing my computer now."

"Be safe, doc."

She hung up as I was pulling Brain's file up and located his contact on my zoom list. Brain Dunaway. A good, honest, hardworking man. Until about four months ago, that is. Brain became a widower and is now the sole provider for his fifteen-year-old step-daughter. Brain came to me to help with grief counseling, but then started telling me how he thought Danella was out of control. I tried to explain to him that she was grieving just as much as he was and to give her some space. At a later appointment, he told me that it just seemed to make things worse. He said he tried to confront her about her reckless behavior. Now, he swears she tries to advance on him sexually.

"Listen, doc, I don't think I'm all that crazy here. Danella is too wild. She's wearing clothes Miranda would have never approved of. Sometimes, when she knows that it's just the two of us in the house, she wears almost nothing. What am I to do, doc?"

"Brain, I think you are over-reacting. Miranda hasn't been gone four months yet. You both are still in the early stages of grief."

"That's just the thing, doc. I don't think Danella is grieving her mother at all. What if she advances on me and I can't resist her?"

"Then, I suggest you both go to some family counseling. This is not healthy for either one of you, Brain."

Jethro walked in and saw me with a client and quietly slipped into the bedroom to change. He was covered in fresh sweat telling me he went a couple rounds with the poor boy. Brain went on and on about how he thought Danella needed to be with someone else while they grieved but I wasn't so sure.

"Listen to me, Brain. It sounds like your anxiety has built up a fine case of paranoia. I'm going to send something to Dr. Snyder for a strong prescription to help you out with all of this, alright. Then, I want you to sit down and have a grown-up conversation with Danella. She's fifteen. She's plenty old enough for you to voice these fears with. Plus, she may be going through something, too, but just doesn't know how to voice them. I'll make us an appointment for two weeks and you tell me how that medicine is doing and how the talk with Danella went, alright."

"Alright, doc. You may be right. Maybe I am just being paranoid. Thanks for seeing me so late, doc."

"Of course, Brain. Get some sleep and tomorrow, go pick up that medication. E-mail me if you need anything."

Once the call ended, I put my computer on the coffee table and leaned my head back, closing my eyes. I felt Jethro's hands on my shoulders as he rubbed the tension out of them.

"I do not know how you do it."

"There are some days, I'm not even sure how I do it."

He smirked as he came around and sat with me. He was in a pair of basketball shorts and still smelled of sweat and the gym. He pulled me to him and I leaned my head on his shoulder.

"Everything go okay with Shane?"

"Yeah. For now, at least. The cops agreed to let him do the program only because I mentioned your name. His mother wasn't too happy about that, but I told her it was no extra charge. Then, Shane insisted he didn't need a shrink poking through his brain. So, I challenged him to a couple rounds. If he could get me down once, we'd talk about the shrink stuff. If he could make me tap out, no shrink. Just fighting"

"What happened, then?"

"Kid's got a lot of built-up tension and he's got strength behind him, but he doesn't know how to use it. After three rounds, he tapped out and agreed to the shrink stuff. You sure you want to handle that?"

"Of course. If I can help you get to the root of these kids' problems, who knows?"

"I agree. After that call...."

"Maybe we should get Danella into your program."

He chuckled at this as I relaxed against him, letting his warmth surround me. I didn't even know I dozed off. I woke up some time later in his bed and he was snoring softly beside me. I smiled to myself before getting up. I went to the kitchen and grabbed a bottle of water before sitting in front of my computer. I turned on the TV, muted the volume, then began sorting through all of my e-mails. Most were client or potential client e-mails that I would respond to tomorrow. I was convinced they were all client e-mails and was about to shut it down when I saw his name. Elliot. My skin felt ice cold and like it was crawling and I was tempted to just delete it, but curiosity got the better of me.

Subject: Please Forgive Me

Body:

I know after everything I've done, you don't want to hear from me. That's why I'm emailing you, though. I'm asking if you think it'll ever be possible that you might be able to forgive me? I would like to meet up sometime, maybe buy you a coffee or lunch to talk about things. Please, Selena. I really am sorry about everything I put you through. All of it. Get back to me, okay?

I just stared frozen at the computer screen. How could he ever think I could forgive him for what he did to me? I was shaken in that thought that I didn't hear Jethro get up and walk in. He touched my shoulders, making me jump.

"What is it?"

Without a word, I showed him the e-mail from Elliot. I couldn't help but laugh as Jethro deleted it. He set aside my computer and lifted me into his arms again. He carried me back to the bedroom and at first, I thought we would continue what we started earlier. Instead, he laid me under the covers and crawled in behind me, pulling me close to him. The feel of his arm curled around me gave me such a sense of peace and security I never thought I needed. I ended up going back to sleep, content in his arms.

Ch.12

The next two weeks passed by in a flash as Jethro and I got into a comfortable routine. I saw all my clients via online appointments only. All new possible patients had to wait a few more weeks unless it was a dire emergency. Jethro started going to the gym more frequently as the time passed. He had a fight coming up in New York he was training for. Brain Dunaway called me back. Said the medicine worked great. He's never felt any better. He also told me he talked to Danella and they were better than ever, though he wouldn't go into detail. I wanted to recommend family counseling, but he refused. He even asked me if they would stop this new medication if he stopped talking to me. He was convinced all his problems were solved since him and Danella talked. I didn't like that sound of that considering what Brain's fears were.

I went to the gym twice a week with Jethro to see to his trouble kids. We spent an hour out their three-hour session with Jethro to talk. Turned out that Shane wasn't a problem child as everyone thought. The kid was acting out because his dad had been sent back to prison. A twenty year sentence this time with no chance of parole. I felt bad for the kid. I did tell him that if he stayed out of trouble, kept to the program, he could help his dad while he was locked up and set up frequent visits with him. In fact, I told him I would look into what could be done and convince Mr. Calloway to have therapy appointments with me for Shane. Shane liked this idea and was excited and even said maybe shrinks weren't all that bad. I shared these ideas with Jethro and he thought it wasn't a bad idea. Most of his trouble kids had some family in jail or prison.

If my plate wasn't full enough due to working from home, things got slightly worse. Elliot actually showed up at my apartment. My neighbor had no idea who he was and told him truthfully that I was staying at Jethro's place. She ended up giving him the address and he huffed over. When I heard the knock, I thought it was Julia. She was already on her way over. After seeing him, I tried to slam the door in his face, but he stuck his foot in the door. He was trying to convince me to open it and let him in while he was pushing the door open. I wasn't sure how long I keep him out like this. He was persistent and I knew he didn't like the idea of me being with Jethro. When I heard Julia come through the elevator, I sighed with relief. She slapped on cuffs and called local uniforms to come pick him up. She was charging him with attempted breaking and entering and harassment. Before she walked out, she assured me that from now on she would call when she was on the elevator or at the door. I gave her a tense and shaky smile before watching her leave and locking the door.

I climbed into the shower and leaned up against the wall as hot water rolled all over me, numbing my skin in the process. I knew Julia would tell Jethro, but I had no idea he would show up so soon. When I felt him climb in behind me and kissed my shoulder, I broke. If he hadn't pulled me to him, I would have collapsed on the shower floor. He held me in an intimate, but non-sexual gesture that spoke volumes to me. I cherished the closeness of his skin against mine. After Elliot literally blindsided me, I wasn't sure I wanted or even could be alone right now. I turned in his embrace, letting the water cascade down my back. I rested my head on his chest and he held me close like that until the water ran cold. He wrapped me in a towel, slipped a pair of boxer briefs on, and just held me on the bed. His voice was stern, yet calming when he finally did speak.

"You know, I still have that cabin outside the city. We can always go there for a bit, if you wanted to."

I was relieved by the suggestion, but for some reason I still felt compelled to ask.

"Are you sure?"

I could feel his smile in my hair as he kissed the top of my head.

"Of course. You are mine now. I'll do anything to take care of you."

I closed my eyes and tried to fight back tears. I was grateful to have him. He was possessive over me, but for some reason it wasn't bad like other relationships were. Maybe this could work.

"I have to call Julia and let her know."

He sat up and got out of bed, retrieving my phone from the living room.

"Call her. I'll pack a few things."

He kissed me tenderly and disappeared into the next room. I didn't much feel like calling Julia, afraid she was still at the station with Elliot. I sent her a quick text.

-Going to Jethro's cabin for a bit. I'll let you know when we get there. XOXO-

I got up and got dressed. I was hoping by going to the cabin, I could avoid Elliot and my stalker. I heard my phone chirp. A return text from Julia.

-That sounds like a good idea. Sucks you'll be so far away, but you need the quiet. Be safe. XOXO-

Jethro was taking a few bags to the car. Even though it was in an underground garage, he told me to wait until he had the car packed and he would come get me. I felt the warmth spread through me at his protectiveness. I smiled at finally making the right choice.

Ch.13

I sat outside the condo building. What else could I do? I needed to see her. Research to find this guy had proven fruitful. She was being hid by one Jethro Knight. He owned the gym, but he was also a UFC fighter. Good choice, my angel, but not enough to overcome me. If it were Michael, maybe, but we both know the Father would never let Michael roam about like us. Not his precious archangel that wanted you that you gracefully chose me over.

I watched people walk in front and go inside, come back out, and go inside, and over again. I sat wondering if any of them saw my angel. Special Agent Kniles pulled up. The defensive look on her face as she approached a car made me sit up in attention. I got out at the same time she bolted inside. I stopped just shy of the doors. What was I thinking? Seattle PD pulled up and I walked a few steps down the sidewalk. Agent Kniles brought out a man struggling against cuffs, pleading with her. I caught the tail end of the conversation.

"Julia! Please! I just want to talk to her!"

"Forget it, Elliot! After what you did to her?! I told you I want you nowhere near my sister!"

I barely remember them putting him in the back of the car. I was seething with rage. What had this man done to my angel? I knew I wouldn't stop until I found out. Rest easy, my angel. Your fighter will protect you for now, but I will make sure you never need protecting.

Inside my apartment, I roared my computer to life. I searched everything I could about this Elliot and my angel. Demon rage consumed me as I read on. Elliot beat my angel beyond recognition. She caught him with another woman in her bed and threatened to have them both removed. The woman fled, so they say, but Elliot beat her. She was rushed to the hospital and rushed straight back to surgery. The reports say she was there for weeks. So, this was also the event that brought Julia back to Seattle? Oh, Elliot, the fun I'm going to have with you! No one touches my angel. NO ONE!

Days went by as I waited outside his building and the police department. No sign of him yet. I found myself back at Jethro's building, but there was longer any sign of him or even Agent Kniles. This Elliot did more to my angel than physically hurt her since they felt the need to move her. Worry not, my dear angel, I will make it safe for you to return. I will eliminate every threat against you if I have to. Bet your fighter couldn't say as much?

I waited for Elliot, letting my anger and rage stew. Agent Kniles must be frustrated with the lack of bodies not showing up now. Trail had gone cold. I wanted all this rage saved for Elliot. I was going to do some of my best work on him. Maybe then, my angel might remember me. Jethro couldn't stand a chance once she remembered me and then, I'd make her forget about this Jethro Knight.

Ch.14

Jethro brought me to the cabin three weeks ago. It's almost Halloween, but I won't be celebrating. I have enough real monsters to deal with. Plus, Jethro doesn't celebrate the holidays. Something about all of them being pagan. He's really convincing once you get him going. Halloween is a pagan holiday anyway, but I'll pass. I know what real nightmares look like.

The air outside was chilly, being late October. I sat on the back deck in one of the oversized oak chairs, curled up with a blanket, sipping my hot green tea. There was no one around for miles. No voices. I didn't have to think or concentrate to block out any sound. The only noise heard was the soft sounds of surf down below as the waves crawled up the beach and then retreated again into the North Pacific. I heard Jethro's motorcycle coming up the mile long drive. I smiled to myself. I truly loved him. I sat right where I was, content, knowing he'd find me. I heard the sliding glass back door open and I felt his eyes on me. I turned slightly in my chair to see his lazy smile stretch across his face.

"What?"

"Nothing. You just look so.... content."

I returned his smile before turning back around.

"I am. It's so peaceful here."

He came around and sat in the matching chair next to me; a serious look now across his features.

"We could stay. Out here, I mean. We don't have to move back to the city."

I just sat stunned. Sure, I had had the idea myself over the past week, but for Jethro to voice it out loud was a huge step. We've only been together for two months and granted it's better than every relationship I've had put together, but......he was talking about making an official move in together.

"The commute would be impossible."

An excuse if I ever heard one and Jethro knew it.

"We own our own businesses. We arrange the hours to fit the new commute time."

"Jethro...."

"I know it's a big step. I just want to keep you safe and I want you to be happy, Selena."

He still saw the hesitation on my face and grabbed my free hand.

"Tell me what's wrong."

"I don't......"

"Look, you like it out here. don't you?"

"Of course. I love it out here."

He smiled and nodded.

"And you sort of like me, right?"

I gave him a playful smile of my own.

"You know I love you, Jethro."

"Then, let's just stay out here."

"Our places in the city?"

He shrugged, like it was an easy answer.

"List them."

"You've been thinking about this, haven't you?"

"Yes. You know I think about long term plans, Selena."

He stood up, then, kissed me, and told me to think about it as he disappeared inside. I stayed where I was until the sun went down and the cold was nipping at me. I grabbed my empty cup and the blanket and walked back inside. I could hear Jethro's game system going and shook my head. I needed to call Julia anyway. I reached for my phone and I was surprised to see she was calling me.

"Hey, Jules. You must've known I was about to call you. I need some advice."

"Of course. What's going on?"

"Jethro asked me to move out here with him."

"Really?! That's....perfect. I mean, you love out there. What advice did you need from me?"

"Just seeing if you think I should."

"Absolutely. Elliot got out yesterday, too, so...."

"That makes it easier. Thanks. Is that why you called?"

"Yeah. Just checking up on you. Haven't heard from either one of you in a bit."

"Well, sorry about that. Got a lot going on, too. You should come up here. You'd love it."

"Maybe. Once this case is over with, at least."

"How's that going?"

"Not good. The trail is still cold. It's like he's gone dormant or something."

"Maybe moved on?"

"Maybe. We found his handy work down by the docks a few days ago, but it's weeks old. Drug dealers mostly. Convenient, I suppose, for him."

"You'll catch him, Jules. I know you will."

"Thanks. I got to run. Just got the laundromat footage this morning. Got to start again somewhere, you know."

"Yeah. Be safe, Jules. I'll talk to you soon."

"Always. You take care of yourself, too, Se."

She hung up before I could confront her. She never called me Se. Not unless something was really wrong. I remember the night mom and dad died.

Don't be sad, Se. They've gone to Heaven. I'll still take care of you.

Jethro came out and saw the uneasy look on my face.

"What happened?"

"Julia just called. Wanted to check in."

"So...."

"She called me Se, Jet."

Jethro nodded his head in understanding. There wasn't anything Jethro didn't know about me. We met eighteen years ago when he transferred to our school. He's been there for me ever since. My forever best friend that I was hopelessly in love with. How could I not. He's sweet, funny, can be asshole but it's cute, he would never hurt me physically, emotionally and mentally; sometimes I think we are equally matched. He understands me. He can read me like no other. The slightest change in my voice or my facial expression and he knows what's wrong without me saying it. He's drool worthy handsome, plays a guitar, rides a motorcycle, a UFC fighter, so he stays fit. He's the one person I feel like I can be myself with. Especially with our shared abilities and visions. I trust him, I feel safe around him. Secure. Like no one can get to me as long as he's by my side. When he holds me, I feel like no one can ever hurt me again. I'm truly happy with him. Thinking about him, how much I love him, still sends butterflies through my stomach. I get this giddy, excited feeling when I hear him come home. He's my favorite person to be around. He's a dork and he's goofy in front of me just to make me laugh. He's tender and stern at the same time. A take charge kind of guy. Like a, 'I'm the boss' sort. He's put up with me all these years, watching me get my heart broke and get beat down time and time again knowing he loved me, but refused to leave. I can never forgive myself for that. Now, he's mine and I am his from this point forth until our last days. I won't give him up. I'd be stupid to. Moving in with him now just seemed so perfect. So right. I smiled up at him and kissed him. The look on his face said sometimes he wished he could read my mind.

Ch.15

I waited and waited for Elliot outside the police station. Finally, I watched as he emerged. I followed silently behind him as he walked towards the bar. I wouldn't let him make it that far. I hit him behind the head and went slack. I hoisted him over my shoulder and walked down the alleyway. The abandoned train yard was a couple miles off. Once there, I threw him down with a resounding thud. I hung the shop light up in the empty car. I splashed water on his face until he woke up sputtering. He squinted his eyes at the light. Once he could see clearly, confusion filled his features.

"Who the hell are you?"

"Your worst nightmare. I plan on causing you unimaginable and unbearable pain."

"What?! What the fuck did I ever do to you?!"

"You hurt my angel. She has left the city because of you."

"Your angel?"

"Of course. How rude of me. You know her as Selena."

I saw his shocked horror as the realization hit him. I couldn't help but grin as he started to beg.

"Wait! Please! I paid for what I did. Spent a couple years in prison for it. I've been trying to make it right to her!"

"Make it right? You hospitalized her for weeks and you think you can make it right to her?!"

"Who the fuck are you, anyway?"

I smiled and nodded my head. Why not tell him? It's not Like I was letting him leave here alive.

"I'll tell you. Only because you won't see the morning."

"Man, please!"

"Hush, now. I am Special Agent Kniles' serial killer. In the flesh."

I did a mock bow. When I caught his face, he had gone pale with sickening terror. He knew what I was capable of. I saw the despair fill his eyes as he began to fidget for a way out. This was going to be fun. I pulled my phone out, which had the stolen hospital records.

"Shall we begin?"

"PLEASE! I'M BEGGING YOU!"

I tsked at him as I gave him a sinister smile. I began to read the records to him.

"Wednesday, October 15, at 6:27 p.m., Dr. Selena KNiles was rushed in by ambulance. At first, we thought she was a victim of a car accident. We were horrified to learn her injuries were a result of a domestic violence. On first observation, we could tell Dr. Kniles had several bruises and lacerations on the surface of her exposed skin. Not a place was left untouched on her face, arms, and legs. After removing her clothing, the damage was more severe. She had deeper bruises to the skin, most likely to the bone. Her hands were fractured. They appeared to be defensive injuries. Her left wrist was sprained and she had two broken fingers. She had two cracked ribs on her right side and one on the left. Her left knee was shattered and the right one suffered from a fractured knee cap. Both feet suffered from defensive wounds as well. Her jaw was dislocated and she had two slipped disks on her back. Her eyes were swollen shut from the bruising. Her mouth was three times its normal size due to the cuts and bruising on it and her nose was also broken. Dr. Kniles was brought to surgery to fix what could be done on her back, jaw, hands, and knees. Dr. Kniles has been placed into a chemically induced coma to give her body a chance to recover. Agent Julia Kniles, the victim's sister, has been contacted and is on the way from Virgina. One Jethro Knight has been approved by family to act as representative until Agent Kniles arrives."

I looked up and met his eyes. By the look on his face, I knew my eyes were the demon black. I saw him shiver when I set the phone down. I picked up a metal bat and swung on his left knee. He howled in pain as I beat it until it shattered.

"I will do everything you did to her and then some."

I didn't give him a chance to respond. I beat both of his knees until I could no longer hear or feel the bones beneath my bat. His screams only angered me. Did my angel scream like this and beg him to stop? I recreated every injury first before putting my own touch to it. By the time I was done, I imagined his insides being mush and he appeared to be a broken marionette puppet sitting there limp. His screams stopped a while ago. I had caved his skull in. I hadn't meant to, but I imagined my angel screaming and trying to get away from him.

I felt more relief than I had in such a long time. My angel had been avenged. I pulled out his phone and texted Julia. It was risky, sure, but I wanted him to be found tonight. I wiped the phone clean and shattered it before throwing it at his lifeless body. My angel would know she was safe now. As I headed home, I swelled with pride. She would see and know it was me and come home to me.

Ch. 16

I was going through the security footage from the laundromat. The picture wasn't really clear. My phone chirped and I was hoping it was Selena. Anger heated me to the core as I saw it was from Elliot.

-Can you meet me in the empty train car. It's an emergency. -

I rolled my eyes, but got up to go. I had two uniforms follow me. Hopefully, he was doing something stupid and illegal. Once we got there, I was horrified. One of the uniforms got sick. I called it in to my unit and the uniforms called it in to get the scene blocked off. Elliot was beaten and disfigured. The M.E. got there to give me a time of death. Based on the body temperature in reference to the text, the killer texted me. I felt a chill crawl up my spine. This was our guy. Why wait weeks just for Elliot? I almost got sick as I put the pieces together. I was betting that if I put the laundromat footage next to Selena's security footage of her stalker, they would match. I almost cried at realizing that my serial killer was Selena's stalker. I put her in his path. He was there at the park that day and at the crime scene the next day. My first thought was to call her and tell her. How could I? Guilt twisted in my gut like a knife as I dialed her.

I almost broke when she answered the phone. She sounded so happy. Jethro was doing something right. There was no way I could tell her now. As I hung up, I made a mistake. I called her Se. I only call her that if something devasting is going on or happened. I only hoped and prayed she didn't catch it. She'd running back and I needed her to stay far away. I needed to figure something out. With this new lead, at least we knew what he looked like. We still didn't have a name, but it was more than we did have. I would do everything in my power to catch him. I wouldn't let this sick, sadistic, son of a bitch get anywhere near my sister. I now only hoped I got to him before he got to her.

I felt that many sleepless nights were in front in me. I wouldn't feel normal again until I had this guy put away.

Ch. 17

The next morning, Jethro drove me into the city with him. He knew I wouldn't stop until I got answers. Something was wrong and Julia wasn't telling me. It worried me too much. Why would she call me Se? Jethro dropped me off and told me to call him. I walked in and the receptionist greeted me warmly.

"Good morning, Dr. Kniles."

"Good morning, Jessica. I'm assuming my sister is in."

"Of course. She's been here all night."

"Thanks."

I walked to the elevator and went up the to fourteenth floor. I head straight the back where her office was. She was passed out on the couch. I grabbed some coffee and woke her up. She was startled and went pale as she saw me.

"Selena! What are you doing here?"

"Making sure everything is okay. Did you honestly think I didn't hear you call me Se?"

"Selena, it was nothing. I've just a lot going on."

She kept rambling on, but I dipped into her thoughts.

Damn it! I knew she caught that! Why couldn't she have just called me again? Why did she have to come back to the city? It's not safe. She just doesn't know the danger she's in. Then, there is the Elliot issue...

Not meaning to, I blurted out after that.

"What Elliot issue?!"

Julia stopped short, looking dumbfounded, then became flushed with anger.

"Selena! You promised never to do that!"

"I wouldn't have to if you'd just tell me the truth. What Elliot issue?"

"Elliot was killed last night. Brutally."

"What?"

"We found him in the old train yard. It was our guy. Maniac actually texted me from Elliot's phone after he killed him so he made sure I would find him. Selena, there is something I need to tell you, okay?"

"Okay."

"Our guy tortured Elliot before killing him. I pulled the security footage from outside Jethro's place the day I arrested Elliot. Out of curiosity. Our guy took a break while Elliot was in jail, so it made sense. Then, I added up some other things. The day we found Thomas; he killed five people in the same day."

She looked at me with a sad, long, look and took me by the hand.

"The security footage from Jethro's, the laundromat footage, and your office security footage all show the same man."

I went pale as fear coursed me. I knew what it meant, but to hear her say it...

"Are you saying...that...that my stalker...is..."

"Oh, Selena, it's all my fault. Had I never brought you on board..."

"NO! Don't think like that. He would have found me eventually. With his obsession with me, at least you know what he looks like. You can find and catch him, right?"

"Yes, of course. Since his fixation on you, he has been sloppy."

"Then, catch him. I'll stay at the cabin, but you get him."

"I will. I promise."

She hugged me tight and I called Jethro. I told him everything Julia had learned. An hour later, he was by my side, still sweating from his workout. His arms engulfed me and I closed my eyes as the sense of security I felt washed over me. He agreed that I should stay at the cabin until further notice.

Julia walked us out and hugged me again. She promised me that she would update as often as she could. Chills ran up my spine as I heard his voice again in my head. I block it out as I climbed into the car and Jethro checked for an opening. Neither of us ever saw the truck. It connected with the front driver's side bumper. Our car went flying and landed with our top on the other parked cars. The truck landed on its side, blocking all traffic. I could feel glass in my mouth as I heard Julia's horrified screams. Everything went black, but not before I heard him: *NO! MY ANGEL!*

Ch.18

I just knew killing Elliot would work! It was probably dangerous for me to be in front of the FBI building, but I knew this is where she would come. To Julia. I watched as Jethro dropped off my angel and drove away. I waited several hours while she was inside. I idly watched as traffic zipped by at dangerous speeds. I grinned. An accident was sure to happen. I sat up, curious, as Jethro pulled back up and hurried inside. Not long after, all three emerged next to Jethro's car. Jethro held my angel as if she were terrified of the world. I whispered to her again and this time she froze and tried not to glance around. Did she hear me? She climbed into Jethro's car as Julia watched from the sidewalk. I stood and watched Jethro scan for an opening in the chaotic traffic. He started to pull out. He should have waited. I watched in pained horror as a truck sped down the road and collided with their car. Glass and metal hitting each other filled the air. Julia screamed and time stood still. I found myself rooted to my spot. Agents rushed out and blocked off the street and contained the scene. EMTs and fire emergency rescue teams rushed on scene. Jethro's side of the car took the brunt of the impact. Angel's side was blocked by the other cars when it flipped. Julia's partner, Jake, held her as she cried in a panic.

EMT's pulled Jethro out and loaded him on the stretcher. He was still breathing. Pity. They examined the car to find a way to get my angel. Was she still alive? I watched as a fire fighter maneuvered himself inside the car. I held my breath. I heard a shout from the man and EMTs rushed with a stretcher. Other fire fighters surrounded the car and angel was carefully lifted out. Relief flooded me. She was still alive, barely. I didn't know what to do. How could I save her?

I went back to my apartment. Inside, I hit my knees and screamed. I demanded to know why. Why did He keep doing this to me? To us? I loved her. Why wasn't that enough? I could do nothing but pace back and forth as I felt the anger build up in me. I felt the anguish rise in my heart and I took it out on anything I could get my hands on. I polished off bottle after bottle of whiskey, rum, and everything else I had. It didn't help to numb anything. I sat and cried on my floor. I knew there would be an accident today. Why did it have to be her? I couldn't...I can't lose her. Not again. I just got my angel back. I need her.

Between tears of pain and anguish and the alcohol, time blurs together. I'm finally numb. I can't even feel her anymore. I don't want to be here without her. Why won't you let me die? The pain is too much. I try suicide, knowing I can't die. After every failure, the pain in my chest doubles. If I were truly to lose my angel this time, will there ever be a chance to get her back again?

Don't go, angel. Please. I need you. Don't take her from me. I'll change. Just give me a chance. Let her pick, again. I'm begging you.

Ch.19

Darkness. Silence. I'm surrounded by darkness and numbing silence. There's only a chill in my bones. Am I dead? Is this what death is like? There's something in the distance. I don't know what I can do, but I try to walk towards it. What I see is astonishing. A landscape as old as time itself. There are no paved roads or cars or anything modern. There's only dirt, grass, and small stone houses. I see a group of children standing near a tree on the outside of this village. I walk closer to them, curious. I stop as I see...myself. I think. It looks like me, but different. I'm in a long flowing white dress knelt in front of the children. My hair is longer and curled and it drapes down my back. I gasp and step back as in an instant, I have white and silver wings that appear from my back. The children cry as the touch them. I notice now standing behind me is a man. If I had to describe him, it's exactly what I would say the archangel, Michael, would look like. Battle hardened, muscled, with a sword strapped to him. Black wings are folded behind him as it seems he stands guard over me and the children. He turns slightly and I see his face. Tears spring to my eyes as it's Jethro's face.

Everything goes black again and I'm left shaken. I have no time to recover as the scene in front of me lights up again. A battle. There's fire, smoke, yelling, and so much blood. I find myself standing in a field as a foul order surrounds me. On one of the fields, I see men in chainmail being coaxed by demons on their backs. The other is where I see myself. God's chosen people and the angels. I remember reading about something like this in the Old Testament. The battle scene fades. I'm facing myself once again. I'm fighting, sword in hand. The demon I face is crafty and swipes at my knee with a dagger. I go down. I hear Jethro/Michael scream. The demon puts the sword to my neck and I look up at him, ready to die. Jethro/Michael runs for me. The demon sneers and he makes us disappear in a puff of smoke. What just happened? My question is answered as I face a cave and I walk up to it. Inside, I am shocked. I am actually making love to the demon. Why...why would I...? I get a good look at the demon and feel sick to my stomach. He looks just like my stalker. I feel a tingling inside me as I watched. He's branded me as his own. I've been ruined, disgraced.

Darkness swallows me this time and I can't see a thing. I can hear a voice, though, along with my own.

"Do you regret your actions?"

"No."

"Serenity?"

Serenity? Is that my name? And I did this?

"I love the demon, Father."

"You know what I must do?"

"Yes. I am not afraid."

Pain shoots through me along my back. Did I just lose my wings? I hear more voices. Jethro's and the one I called Father.

"I can't...not without her!"

"She has chosen, Michael. You are needed home. You must forget her."

"I can't."

"I promise you, when the time is right, I will send you to her."

"I..."

Then, I see Michael. He stands before the demon. I can't see myself.

"I promise you, Malachi, you will not keep her."

"I've won, Michael. Face it. She's mine."

"Not for long. I'd rather see her dead then see her with the likes of you."

"Michael..."

Darkness fades in. My heart is racing. What happened? I died. The archangel's request was fulfilled. So, was this my second chance? The time Father said would be time for Michael. After all, he is Jethro. What is an archangel doing chasing someone like me here on earth? Why waste the time?

I hear beeping noises around me and I still see darkness. I try to open my eyes. I'm still trying to process what I've seen and heard. I feel constricted, like I'm tied down. I begin to panic as I can't move. Blinding light fills my vision. I hear Julia next to me, but I can't make out what she's saying. What's happening? Where am I? I try blinking a few times, forcing my eyes to focus. I can see Julia now. I try to say something. but I can't. Something is in my throat. A doctor and some nurses come rushing in. The doctor checks my vitals and smiles. He says something, but I can't hear him. A nurse appears next to him. I feel like gagging as she leans over me and I realize she's just pulled out a breathing tube. Why did I have a breathing tube? The grogginess has faded away a bit and the room comes into full focus. I'm in the hospital, intensive care. I'm confused. The doctor fills my vision again.

"Can you hear me, Dr. Kniles?"

I nod my head in response. He walks me through basic motor skills. I decide to test my voice.

"What happened to me?"

The doctor glances at Julia and gives her a tight smile and a sharp nod before walking out. Julia scoots closer to the bed and grabs my hand.

"You don't remember anything?"

I shake my head.

"You and Jethro were in a terrible car accident."

My eyes go wide with panic. Where is Jethro?

"You almost didn't make it. It's been three weeks. Though Jethro's side took the hit, when the car flipped, you ended up wedged between your door, the pavement, and some other cars. They were lucky they could get you out."

Fear has my voice as I try to say Jethro's name. Thankfully, Julia understands.

"Jethro is okay. He's been awake for two days now. He's really worried about you. I check in on him, too. He was in here last night. He's in worse shape than you, though. Like I said, his side took the brunt of the impact."

I wince in pain at a sudden muscle spasm and Julia goes to get something for pain.

Two weeks go by and I still can't see Jethro. One night, I test to see if I can walk. I can't go far but there's a wheelchair in the room. I manage to get to it and wheel myself to Jethro's room four doors down the hall. He's asleep when I roll in, but wakes up when I get next to the bed. He smiles at me and grabs my hand. He looks awful. I want to tell him about what I saw, but how? What if he wasn't shown anything? I decide I'll wait until he recovers more to tell him.

The next morning, I got caught in his room as the doctor and Julia look for me. I'm going to be discharged and Jethro insists I stay at the condo. I start to protests, but Julia says if I don't, I have to stay with her. What choice did I have? I agree to stay at the condo. Jethro squeezes my hand. He's scared for me. I promise him that I'll come see him every day until he's discharged. He relaxes a bit.

For the next week, the images of Serenity play through my mind at night. Jethro knows something is wrong, but I refuse to tell him anything. Not yet. One night, it hit me like a cold blast of wind and everything became so clear to me. Malachi has been trying to reach me. He even killed Elliot for what he did to me. Oh, Malachi. I need to find you. But how? I can't ask Julia if she's had any new leads. She'd never tell me anyway. How could I be so stupid? It all made sense now. I remember every time he got into my head. Could I get into his? I sat cross-legged on the bed and concentrated on Malachi. Images filled my mind's eye. I could feel what he was feeling. Hate, anger, despair, and extreme sorrow. He had wandered the earth, looking for me. He has killed women he hoped were me and in a fit of rage and disappointment, killed them. I feel pleasure from him in the moment of the kill but it's replaced by crushing loneliness. I try to focus more on his location. Where are you, Malachi? I see a room, an apartment. I know where this is. It's across the city. I bolt up, not really having a plan. I hailed a cab and give him directions to the apartment building. Once I'm standing outside, I feel nervous. I knocked on his door. No answer. I fetch the building manager and explain that Malachi is a patient of mine and he lets me inside. The place is trashed. There are holes in the drywall, empty bottles across the floor, and the furniture is overturned. He saw my accident. I remember hearing his voice right before I blacked out. Did he think I was dead? Where are you, Malachi? Outside again, I try to focus once more on him. Specifically, his pain. I see water, warehouses. The Seattle Docks! I hail another cab. At the docks, the driver is hesitant to leave me alone. I convince him I'm meeting someone. A cop. I watch his tail lights disappear. I take a deep breath. Alright, Malachi, where are you? I can feel him. I'm nervous, but I walk towards the warehouses. I take another deep breath and scream his name.

Ch.20

Is it possible for someone like me to lose their mind? I start to think it is possible, but maybe not my mind. Perhaps the heart I'm not even supposed to have. For the first week, she's still in a coma with no change to her condition. Week two, I feel the pain in my chest as I want to die all over again as she had complications and had to be rushed back to surgery. By week three she's improving, but still in a coma. She has a breathing tube stuck in her throat. I'm worried, though. She's been taken off the drugs keeping her under, but she still isn't close to coming out of her coma. Why won't she wake up? I can't stand it. It feels like my angel is slipping away. Worst of it is I can't even be near her. Julia hardly ever leaves her side. I know one thing, I can't stay here anymore.

I took a trip to the Canadian wilderness. Maybe the snow will do me some good. As two more weeks blends into three, I find I am enjoying myself. No is safe from me. Hikers, campers, hunters, tourists, cops, and even the animals fall prey to my rage. The mess I have left in my wake would have Julia and her crew at the FBI in a frenzy. Being the wild back country, it'll take these Mounties ages to discover what I've done. Even then, it may be blamed on wild animals. My rage has burned beyond my control and I no longer care.

A chill ran through me like an icy blast and I know it's not the elements around me. Angel. She's awake. Not Selena. Serenity. My angel has returned to me. Does she remember me? I waste no time trying to get back to her. Once I return to Seattle, I discover she has already been discharged from the hospital. Now, the question is if she's with Julia since Jethro is still a patient inside. I can't handle this. She is so close, but I can't reach her. I decide to head to the docks. It has become a favorite place of mine to vent recently. Anger is surging through me as I put the pieces together. Jethro or I should say Michael. The archangel son of a bitch is still trying to get her. She chose me the first time and she will choose me again. The guardian can hold onto his mortal memories of the two of them. My rage is burning. I need to kill something. I can't believe Michael tried again.

There's five men for my entertainment. Guns drawn, it's three against two. I feel their confusion before it appears on their faces at my arrival. In my state of rage, it's nothing to overpower them. When they gain a state of consciences again, they are suspended from the chains. I gagged them this time. I don't feel like listening to input. My head is already throbbing. It's an unusual pressure beating against my mind. The center guy is trying to talk seeing my face, but I hush him. Something is going on. I hear something small in the distance, a voice. I walk to the door. It's not just in my head. I hear it again. My eyes go wide as I realize the voice is saying my name. My heart threatens to beat out of my chest. Angel! She came looking for me. I impulsively run out, not even sure where she is. I call out to her.

"SERENITY!!"

"MALACHI!"

I hear the relief in her voice and I almost break. The excitement is almost too most.

"MALACHI!"

"I'm here, Serenity!"

She's close now. I bolt around the corner and I freeze. There she stands, looking perfect. I see her lip tremble and I take off. I need to feel her in my arms. I need to make sure she knows she'll never be alone. She meets me halfway. I scoop her up by the waist as she wraps her arms and legs around me. I breathe in her scent scared this still just a dream.

"My beautiful angel."

My breathless whisper causes chills to spring up on her skin. My heart breaks at her tearful apology.

"I'm so sorry, Malachi. I didn't...I didn't know."

"I know, my love. It's okay. Do not cry. You are with me, now."

We held each other close for what seemed like hours. I grit my teeth as I remember the men inside and turn to go back. She grabs my hands, forcing me to stop.

"Where...?"

"Unfinished business, baby."

"Oh, Malachi, don't."

There it was. My angel had me torn in two. I wanted to go back and finish them but how could I now that she was here.

"They have seen my face, angel."

"Julia has seen your face."

"How?"

"My office, the laundromat, outside Jethro's the day Elliot was arrested. You... you killed him, didn't you?"

I rubbed my thumb across her cheek, tenderly.

"I had to. He hurt you."

"And now? Those men?"

"You want me to let them go?"

"Please, Malachi?"

"I don't..."

"For me?"

I was defeated. I let out a sigh of defeat and nodded. I walked back inside, told them an angel had literally saved them, knocked them out, and returned to my angel. Back outside, I claimed my angel's lips once more as mine and disappeared with her into the night.

Ch.21

"Michael! Wake up! She needs you!"

I bolted upright, but as myself. I could feel it. I find myself trembling in my hospital bed. The accident triggered the memories back. I knew we were fallen angels, but I had no idea I was the archangel, Michael. Did her memories come back, too? It made sense now. That's why she needs me. She ran right for Malachi, her stalker. I needed Julia's help, but how do I go about telling her? I felt my fists clench and I ripped out my IV lines. I ran straight for the condo and cursed when I found it empty. Her phone, purse, and the bed was messed up. Malachi already had her by now. I silently prayed that she would remember that she picked me in this life and that it would actually count for something. I snatched her phone and called Julia, knowing she would have the entire force behind her to track them down.

"Hey, Selena. Is everything okay?"

"Julia, listen to me. Please tell me you know where she is?"

"Jethro? I didn't know they let you out?"

"JULIA! I'm at the condo and she's not here, but her stuff is."

"I don't...you don't think..."

"I do. Julia, we have to find her."

"Meet me here, now."

After hanging up, I drove like a madman straight to the FBI building. Selena can be mad at me later just as long as there is a later. When I got up to her floor, Julia had every available agent, detective, and uniformed cop in Seattle.

"Our serial killer has been identified as my sister's stalker. One who now has her in his grasp. This is our top priority. Please. Help me find my sister before it is too late. We all know his MO. I don't want to be too late."

She dispatched everyone and I left with her. She sent a SWAT team to the docks. I would do anything to save Serenity this time. I would not fail her again. I was not the archangel Michael for nothing and I was determined to make it count this time, even if it costs me my life. I would remind her that she chose me and maybe, just maybe, I could save her in the process. She would be redeemed and we would be together this time.

Ch.22

I was surprised when we didn't go back to his apartment, but then I remembered its state and understood. He drove us towards the edge of town and parked in front of the nicer of the hotels. Every time he looked at me, he couldn't help but smile. He seemed to ooze joy at the notion that he had me again. Yet, why did I not feel the same? I had the memories and I should be happy. Why do I feel so guilty? I felt a nagging that something just didn't feel right. Once we were in the room and alone, he noticed it.

"What is it?"

"It's just...I..."

"It's Michael, isn't it?"

"Malachi, I...."

"I can't believe this! After centuries of being apart, we are finally together again and You Are Thinking About Michael!!"

"Malachi, please. Try to understand. I just feel guilty because he's still in the hospital."

"HE'S A FUCKING ARCHANGEL!"

"That is still mortal. He could die."

"I seriously doubt He will let that happen."

"Malachi?"

"I won't let you go this time, Serenity."

"I will come back."

"You don't get it? You are not leaving me!"

"I have to!"

"And Julia?"

"I'll figure it out."

"NO!!!!"

I turned to run for the door. Fear chilled me to my very core. He was Julia's serial killer after all and I know what he has been capable of before now. He beat me there and I found myself hoisted off the floor against the wall. His hands were like vise grips I couldn't release from around my throat. As my vision started blurring, I prayed Jethro was once again Michael and shouted out to him: *MICHAEL! HELP!*

I was sitting in Julia's car when my mind felt like I was having a brain freeze. Serenity. I heard her voice cry out in my head. I reached back out, hoping I wasn't too late.

Serenity? Where are you?

Michael! Michael, he's choking me...I....

Serenity! Try and focus. I need to see where you are.

Michael....

Suddenly, a room flashed before me. A nice hotel room. The image was faint and going darker and panic surged through me as I realized she couldn't see it anymore. He was killing her. I got out of the car and just ran. I checked three hotels, but none felt right. Finally, I prayed to the Father for guidance to be able to find her. I stopped and didn't know how I ended up at my next stop, but I was thankful. It was the Marriott at the edge of the city. I wasn't sure which room, but I let my feet guide me. I stopped in front of room 326 and burst through. My heart stopped. Malachi was bent over the bed. Anguish from his cries filled the room. I inched closer, not wanting to see that her body was unmoving on that bed.

"Malachi...what...what have you done?"

"I didn't...I got so angry...I...I... Michael?"

I walked to the other side of the bed and felt for a pulse. Nothing. I didn't even realize I had backed up until my back found the wall and I hit my knees. Malachi just stared at me with such hopelessness.

"She's...she's gone."

How could I have failed her yet again?

Ch.23

I came out of Serena's office building to find Jethro wasn't still in the car. I tried calling him, but got nothing. I tracked his phone and saw he was at the Marriott. I didn't even question it. I called all units to that location. Jake got there at the same time I did and we rushed in. Guests are confused as all exits are blocked and ready for any type of escape attempt. We scan every floor. Only on the third floor is there a door that has been kicked in. I nudge it open and freeze. My serial killer is unmoving next to the bed and Jethro is shattered against the wall. Other agents rush in and cuff him and he doesn't even flinch. I start to panic as I see Serena on the bed, unmoving and deathly still. I take her hand in mine once I find the courage to walk to her and find it so cold. Paramedics storm passed me and get to work. I feel the tears fall as they confirm that she has no pulse. I watch as they break out the paddles and set them to charge. Electricity buzzes through her, but she doesn't move. They charge the paddles again, higher charge this time. Nothing. I hit my knees as I can't control the tears anymore and beg God not to take my sister away from me. She's all I have left. They hit again with an even higher charge and a new kind of buzz fills the room. She has a pulse. A faint pulse, but still a pulse. Jethro gets to his feet as they rush her out of the room. He rides in the ambulance with her as I head for the FBI interrogation room. I can't sit in for questioning, but I observe as my partner grills him. It was agreed that we let him think he killed Selena. Even standing here, though, it may not be far from the truth.

On the table in front of him is boxes filled with pictures and paperwork from the last seven years. All his kills. My killer is unmoving, like he doesn't care. Jake starts anyway.

"What do I call you?"

He doesn't even acknowledge him.

"Need to call you something. There is no record of you."

He looks up, slightly.

"Malachi."

"Alright, Malachi. Any place you'd like to start for us?"

He meets Jake's eyes.

"Where is she?"

I feel my jaw clench as anger courses through me.

"Who?"

"My angel?"

"Your angel?"

"Selena."

"Dr. Kniles is no longer with us. It's why I am questioning you and not our lead agent on the case."

"Julia?"

"Yes."

I feel a chill wash over me. How much about us does he know?

"Did I really kill her?"

"Yes. They pronounced her dead on scene."

"I never..."

"Tell me everything."

I feel the anticipation as Malachi sits up straight and doesn't break eye contact with Jake.

"I killed them. All of them. 133 of them before I found angel. I wanted each one of those women to be angel so badly. Discovering they weren't her made me so angry that I just couldn't help myself. They were too easy. When I saw her that day in the park, I knew it was her. When she looked at me like she didn't even know me, well, that really made me angry. I killed the woman outside the restaurant and stuffed her in her trunk but it did nothing for me. After all, I found my angel. The man was next. I felt some relief at his death and it was enough to last me through the night. The next morning, discovering my angel knew the man I had killed, I felt angry with myself. I had hurt her. Anger and jealousy soon replaced this feeling when I saw her with Jethro. The couple on the trail was just random luck. They reminded me of them and I had to try and erase the image from my mind. When my angel moved in with Jethro, I felt betrayed. I tried my best to drink away the hurt, but I couldn't. The homeless woman was an accident. I ended up taking my anger out on the guys at the docks. Vented to them even. Still, it didn't help much. I really had no intention of killing the little old lady at the laundromat, but it happened. She was satisfying to watch. Now, Elliot, on the other hand, I planned out. I found out what he did and just knew I wouldn't let him live. My angel left the city because of him. I was happy with my work. When she came back, I knew it would be different. When the truck hit them, everything went numb. How could I lose her after just getting her back? I took a trip to Canada. Had a lot of fun up there. Your record for 144 kills isn't even close to being the right number. When angel remembered me, I felt it. She came looking for me, though. SHE FOUND ME! I can't tell you the joy I felt at holding her again. Something was wrong. I asked her what it was and she said her coming to me was a mistake. A MISTAKE! BECAUSE OF HIM! After everything I did to get her back and what I've been through, she said I was a mistake. My anger got the best of me and blinded me to her. I didn't realize I had choked her to death until I felt her body go slack. You say she is gone. I killed my angel. Now, I don't really care what happens to me. I am nothing without her."

He sat back and looked to the floor. All of us were stunned. We were hoping to get something, but none of us expected a full confession. This case was finally over. Jake walked in and put a hand on my shoulder.

"Go and see your sister. We will wrap everything up here, Julia."

"Thanks, Jake."

I got to the hospital and found Jethro in the surgery waiting room. He stands up when he sees me.

"They rushed her right to surgery. I was told that her windpipe was nearly crushed."

"Oh my...what did they..."

"The doctor is confident he can fix it."

"Thank God."

"How did it go?"

"He gave us a full confession."

"Good."

Jethro was angry and didn't look like himself, but that was understandable. Malachi was where he finally belonged.

When the doctor came out, we got to our feet.

"Doctor, how is she?"

"We managed to repair the damage to her windpipe. Recovery will be a slow process for her. It could have been a lot worse than it was. We were actually really lucky. I am confident that she will make a full recovery in time."

It was still hours before we could actually see her in her own room. I cried all over again when I saw her. Her entire throat was bandaged and her hands were restrained to the bed. There was a tube at the base of the throat so she could breathe. The nurses said the doctor ordered for her to be in a coma until she had recovered enough. Jethro sat down next to her bed and rubbed the back of her hand. He looked up at me.

"Go on home, Julia. You've had a rough day. I'll notify you of any changes."

"Are you sure?"

"Yes. She's in a coma. Go."

I nodded slowly, not wanting to leave her, but he was right. I started the tiring trip home to try and unwind from the day.

Ch.24

I didn't know what to do. I willed everything inside me to show Michael what he needed to see. Darkness was closing in around me. The pain in my throat was becoming unbearable and I knew Malachi was crushing it. I tried uselessly to get him to let go, but it was like he no longer saw or heard me. I knew I was dead when it seemed like I floated over everything and I saw him kill me. My body had gone limp. Malachi let go and my body slumped to the floor. I saw the panic fill his entire being as he realized what he had just done. He lifted my lifeless body and set it on the bed. He shook me, screaming my name. Tears fell to the bed cover as he knew he had just killed me. I watched with a sadden heart as Michael kicked in the door. I saw the heart-wrenching pain in his eyes as he knew that he was too late. His back hit the wall and he became a mess on the floor. Julia wasn't far behind. The pain she felt was visible from this side. It was awful to witness. Agents took Malachi away, who didn't fight them. I almost cried as EMTs tried to revive me. Once, twice, and still nothing. I cried, though, when Julia hit her knees and prayed. I could hear her prayer in my head as if I were standing right next to her. My gift made sense now. I heard and answered the prayers of those who hurt emotionally. I can't even imagine all those unanswered prayers because I chose Malachi. The EMTS hit me again and I felt it.

At the hospital, I observe my surgery, but not alone. That voice that was in the vision when I got my memories back was there. I've already learned that it is Father. He has a hand on my shoulder as the doctors and nurses work on me.

"He killed me."

"Why do you seem so surprised?"

"I wanted him to understand."

"Malachi was possessive of you. He would have never understood, my dear."

"So, it was all pointless?"

"Yes. But never give up hope. I didn't name you Serenity for nothing."

"Father? Could I have changed him?"

"Perhaps, when he was first created. By the time he found you, though, he was too far gone."

"Michael came back for me."

"Michael would've given everything up for you."

"He has truly earned what he has. I don't deserve him."

"Ask him that. He says something very different. Even now."

"I went back to Malachi and he killed me. It's my fault. How could he possibly..."

"Because he loves you. As do I. And like me, has forgiven you for everything."

"Father, I..."

"Mistakes will always be made. You are guided by your heart. It's what makes you who you are. Tell me something, though. If I gave you your wings back, what would you do?"

"Could I stay here. Finish out this life? I don't think I could leave Julia."

"Of course."

"Michael?"

"I would want him to come back, but I know he'll never leave without you. I will grant him his wings here as well."

"Thank you, Father. Can I ask you something?"

"Anything."

"Why did you wait so long?"

"I waited until I knew you were ready."

Darkness caved in again and I knew my surgery was over. I would live and wake up. How long I would sleep, I wasn't sure. I knew one thing for sure. I was redeemed. I chose Michael and he would be there when I awoke. He'd never leave and I'd never be alone again.

Ch.25

Six Weeks Later...

I could hear beeping and the humming of machines around me. I felt a warmth on my hand. I struggled to open my eyes, but they won't move. I try to wiggle my fingers or do anything, but it's useless. I can't do anything and I'm sore everywhere. I can breathe, but it feels...wrong. I feel panic rising in my mind and the beeping next to me increases in rhythm and sound. It causes the warmth on my hand to vanish. I hear a muffled man's voice and I realize he's trying to calm me down. I attempt to relax as he helps me get my eyes open. I squint at the harsh light and it disappears as someone cut the light off. I blink a few times, adjusting to my surroundings. A doctor is standing just above me. He smiles once he sees my eyes open and fully adjusted.

"Welcome back, Dr. Kniles. I'm Dr. Ferrarro. I'm going to ask you some questions, alright, and I want you to blink for your replies. Blink once for no and twice for yes. Think you can do that?"

I blink twice.

"Wonderful. Now, are you in any pain?"

I blink twice again.

"We will get you something to help with that."

He turns to a nurse and she walks out.

"Do you know what has happened?"

This time, I only blink once.

"Your windpipe was nearly completely crushed. You went through extensive surgeries to repair the damages. You've been recovering in a coma for six weeks."

Six weeks? And what he said about my windpipe. Could it all be true? Wait! How am I breathing, right now? I try to reach a hand up to find out, only I can't. I look down and see my hands restrained to the bed.

"Easy, Dr. Kniles. There is a tube connected to the base of your throat to allow oxygen in and out. In the next few weeks, we might try to take it out and see if therapy will be of use to you to try and get you to breathe properly again. For now, you are still healing. It is still going to take time, but I am hopeful you can make a full recovery from this."

As I watch him walk out, I feel the warmth return to my hand. I look over and attempt a smile as I see Julia with tears in her eyes. I squeezed her hand and she cried more.

"I am so sorry, Se. I should've been there. I shouldn't have left you. I should've kept you safe."

I shake my head.

"I led him to you, Se. It's my fault."

I shake my head again with a pleading look. Before she can say another word, the door opens and everything changes. It's Jethro. He takes my other hand and kisses it. Julia smiles now, and excuses herself. Once she's gone, Jethro points to his head and I listen in.

How are you feeling, Serenity?

I shake my head and he kisses my hand again. The nurse comes in and injects the pain medicine into my IV line and Jethro squeezes my hand as I drift off sleep.

Two months go by and I'm still in the hospital. I've been having regular oxygen therapy for about a week now. They removed the tube this morning and I can breathe on my own. It's a struggle and it feels like sandpaper, but at least I don't need the tube anymore. Plus, my hands are now unrestrained. I've been using my phone to text everyone since I still can't talk. Julia has to be in court today, so Jethro is with me all day.

"Can I ask you something?"

I nod.

"What happened?"

I knit my brows together, not understanding his question.

"When you got your memories back. I want to know what happened. I need to, Serenity."

I nod my head with a saddened look and unlock my phone. He does deserve to know, but not like this.

-I know, but I want to tell you. Not like this. -

"I understand that, but..."

-But... I do want you to know something. -

He looks at his phone and back to me, nervous.

-I chose you. -

"You...what?"

I smile and nod at him. I see him struggle to understand as a smile tore across his face.

-As Selena and Serenity. -

He leaned over and kissed me like never before and I knew he was kissing me as Michael. We both turned as someone cleared their throat at the door. Julia walked in with a smile on her face.

"Should I come back later, then."

"No. Come on in."

Julia sat down next to me and took my hand.

"I thought you'd like to know what is happening with Malachi's case."

I gulp, but nod my head.

"As you know, we got a full confession. The defense attorney tried saying it was no good based an emotional trauma, but we got that knocked out of the way. they are moving forward with a jury trial, no plea deals. We are trying to get with Canadian officials to see if that part of his confession is true or not."

"Has a trial date been set yet?"

"No. These things take time and the judge wants the report from the Canadians before he sets a date. He has no bond, so no matter what, he's stuck behind bars."

"That's good."

She looks at me with that heartbroken look again. I pulled out my phone.

-Stop. It's not your fault. I'm just glad you caught him. -

"I still blame myself, though."

"Julia, it would have happened eventually. He was her stalker."

"I know, but...forgive me anyway, Selena."

-There is nothing to forgive, but if there was, of course I forgive you. -

She squeezed my hand and smiled. Dinner was arriving; chicken broth. Yuck!

Ch.26

The room was a whirlwind of activity. I was released today. Jethro made sure he had everything he would need for me to stay with him at the condo. I was sure he was never letting me out his sight again. Once we got there, Julia put my hospital instructions as well as my bags on the coffee table while Jethro settled me on the couch. Julia came and sat next to me and Jethro took my bags to the bedroom.

"You feel okay?"

I nod my head and use my hand in a mock gesture of yawning. Her phone rings and she stands up to take it.

"Special Agent Kniles....Yes, sir...Yes, sir...Thank you, sir.... Just walked through the door.... No, sir, I can come in....When do you need me? Of course, sir.... I'm on my way as we speak."

She turned to me with an apologetic look on her face and I waved my hand at her for her to go. Jethro came back into the room just before she left.

"Call me. Seriously. If you guys need anything."

"We will. Be safe."

Jethro locked the door behind her and joined me on the couch.

"What do you need?"

I make the mock gesture again and he smiles. My pain medicine is starting to kick in.

"I have to clean a bit more in there. I'll come get you."

I nod my head and watch him disappear into the bedroom. I relax my head against the back of the couch and end up drifting off to sleep.

I shielded my eyes against the sunlight pouring into the room. I was in bed. Jethro must have carried me in here yesterday. Had I been asleep all night? I looked around and couldn't see or hear Jethro anywhere. I got up out of bed and went to the kitchen. I smiled as I found his note in front of the coffee maker. I read it as I poured me a cup.

I had things at the gym to take care of. I'll try and make it back by lunch. Take it easy today. I'll be back as soon as I can. I love you.

I took my cup and opened my computer. I had so many emails and messages from clients and others wishing I get well soon. Others saying they couldn't believe what happened. Others said they were praying for my speedy recovery. I was exhausted just looking at them all.

With a sigh, I closed my computer and turned on the TV. It was already switched onto the news. All anyone was talking about was Malachi and how they thought he was our generation's version of Jack the Ripper. I was about to switch it off when Julia's face appeared on screen. Every reporter wanted her attention for a question or comment.

"Agent!"

"Agent!"

"Special Agent Kniles! Please! Just one question!"

"One question."

"Tell us, please, how it feels to finally put this monster behind bars."

"I was just doing my job. I spent years tracking him and it paid off. I know the city will sleep soundly once more tonight."

"Agent!"

"Agent! Over here!"

"Nothing further."

Then, she disappeared inside the building with the reports still calling after her. I felt proud of her. She was with me when I did my interviews for the papers and magazines and online blogs.

I got up for another cup of coffee as Jethro walked back in. He took one look at the TV and raised an eyebrow at me.

"You really want to be watching this?"

I jotted something down and smiled at him. I kissed him and handed him the little note.

Julia's Interview

He smiled and nodded his head and continued to the kitchen. He set bags on the counter that I hadn't realized he had before. He gave me an amused look as he pulled out cartons of ice cream. My face lit up. I walked over to him and he lifted me up on the counter. He fixed me a bowl of the coffee flavored ice cream and put the cartons in the freezer. He leaned on the counter and proceeded to watch me tongue fuck the spoon with every bite I took.

Sometime later, Julia let herself in. Jethro had given her a key after I was released. Jethro and I were curled up under a blanket on the couch. She plopped down in the chair and swiped my unfinished bowl of ice cream. She looked at us and laughed as she set the now empty bowl back on the table.

"Sorry. It's been a long day."

"You're fine. She watched your interview on TV today."

"Really? What did you think?"

I clapped my hands in a mock gesture. I pulled out my phone as she smiled at me.

-You were very professional. Seemed like they didn't bother you at all. -

"Thanks. Believe it or not, they put us through training to deal with the media."

-I remember. But you still did good. -

"I actually have to tell you something. It's the reason I came over."

Jethro got up from the couch, grabbed the bowls, and headed for the kitchen. I smiled in his direction before looking back to Julia.

"Quantico wants me back."

-That's wonderful news. What did you tell them? -

"I told them I couldn't make any decision until this case was officially over."

-You are going to take it, though, aren't you? -

"I mean I don't know. Probably not. I made you a promise."

-Oh, no, you don't. This is huge. Don't you dare pass on this because of me. -

"Alright. I still have to think about it. With my break-up with Nate, I think after this case, I want to take some down time."

-Okay, fine. I can see that. But this opportunity is perfect for you. -

"I know."

Jethro walked back over as Julia stood to leave. She hugged me and promised to keep me updated on everything. After she left, Jethro pulled me close to him on the couch. I rested my head on his shoulder as he held me, his warmth comforting me in the process. I started to drift off to sleep and he carried me to bed.

Later that night, as I slept, I felt Malachi's intrusion in my head. Terrible images of what happened flashed across my mind's eye. I jumped up, sweat dripped off my skin like I just got out of a pool. I looked at the clock. 3:45 a.m. I looked over and found Jethro sound asleep. I wipe my forehead and got up and headed to the bathroom. I turned on only the hot water and pointed the shower head towards the wall. I sat on the floor inside the shower as steam filled the bathroom. I hugged my knees to myself and found I couldn't stop shaking. Steam surrounded me but I was still freezing. My mind cried out for Michael.

Michael! I need you!

Next thing I knew, Jethro was turning off the water and wrapping me in an over-sized towel. He cradled me on the bed as he soothed me. I spoke to him through our mind link, now that we could do so.

Why does he still have this hold on me?

He marked you. You need to replace his mark.

I want him out, Jet.

Do you trust me?

You know I do.

He leaned up, un-wrapped the towel, and then started his personal mission to remove Malachi's mark not only from my body and mind, but also my heart and soul.

Ch. 27

She laid in bed, her body still buzzing from the experience. I replayed everything in my mind. My right hand ran through her hair while my left stroked her face, neck, and chest. Occasionally wandering comfortably over the breast within my reach. My kisses making her feel like I was dying of thirst and her mouth held the only water source. I felt so complete. It was as if I had somehow been solved and assembled. I connected the fragments making them tightly interlock in order to show my eyes the gorgeous image I was enjoying. I took in the sight of the way she had lifted and presented herself. As I did, a smile crept across my face before licking my fingers, polishing myself to a shine and making that final piece fit. Raised hairs and a rapid pulse raged through her like wildfire. My mind was ablaze and my fingers were the matchsticks. She had no choice. All she could do was lay there; lay there and burn. That celestial voice echoed between these walls as we made love. My thumb drew halos around her while her body I was slowly sliding in and out of shook and trembled at my touch. The flow I could no longer suppress matched the warmth she held around me. I watched lips quiver and a fair-skinned chest rise and fall heavily. Knowing at that moment something new had been created. She had been given wings in my heart. She was taking her very first breaths after becoming my angel.

I walked back in the room, carrying a cup of coffee for her. Her face is flush and she can't stop the smile from spreading across her face. I walked over and set the cup on the side table. I can't help myself as I smile. Sunlight poured in from open windows. Her nakedness sprawled over the sheets on which we spent night after night dreaming dreams that could never be this lucid. She was still as a bundle of lilacs brought inside from the neighboring bush. Changing the room. Silently making the air more pleasant to breathe. Making the room so much more beautiful and inviting. Making it feel like home. Bringing the world from outside in for me to feel like these walls weren't so confining. I sighed and sat on the bed with her.

"You can't stay in this bed all day. You have speech therapy in a few hours."

Her response was to pull the covers over her head. I let my hand creep under the blanket, feeling the tender flesh I bruised just hours before. I feel the goosebumps raise across her skin. I rub the still slick center and get close to her ear.

"Get up, Babygirl. I promise there will be plenty of time for us to just be in bed together."

She lowered the blanket and her eyes went wide as my fingers hooked inside of her and started to dance. I made promises to her between kisses to her neck.

"In fact," *kiss* "the sooner I get you to the cabin," *kiss* "you won't be able to get out of bed."

I felt her tighten around my fingers as she came in my hand. I sucked on the fingers, tasting her holy water as she stared at me disbelieving. I kissed her shocked expression as I got up. I left the room, still naked and gave her time to get ready.

Jethro left me shocked and breathless as I watched his too handsome naked form disappear from our bedroom. I sat up and drained my cup of coffee before heading to the bathroom. As I washed my hair, I mused about how different I had been just hours before in this room. An hour and a half later, I stepped out in dark jeans, one of his shirts, and my ankle high boots. My hair flowed with beach curls and my make-up was done to perfection. I actually felt like me again. Jethro smiled as he knew he was the reason for my renewed confidence. I stared at him as he took my empty cup to the sink. He had dressed while I showered. He was in faded blue jeans, a t-shirt, and his cowboy boots. I smiled as he could never truly be rid of his Mississippi roots. My phone broke my trance as a text from Julia came through.

-Good luck today. Let me know how it goes. -

I smiled as Jethro grabbed our coats. I grabbed my purse before we walked out.

At the doctor's office, people kept staring. It made me wildly uncomfortable. I was glad when we didn't wait long. Dr. Franklin sat in front of me on the little stool.

"How do we feel today, Selena?"

I make a so-so gesture with my hand.

"Well, hopefully, by the time we are done here, you'll be able to tell me. Are you ready?"

I took a deep breath and nodded my head. It was going to be a long day.

Three hours later, my bandages had been changed and my throat felt like sandpaper. Honestly, it felt like I had screamed for the last three hours. Dr. Franklin said she had taken it slow and easy on me, but it certainly didn't feel like it. Once we were back at the condo, Jethro made me a cup of hot tea, hoping it would soothe the gravel feeling in my throat. I pulled out my phone to let Julia know everything after I sank into the couch.

-Worst three hours of my life. -

-I'm sorry. How bad was it? -

-She said she took it easy on me, but I feel like I screamed the entire time. -

-That sucks. I wish you didn't have to go through it.-

-Me too. -

-So, I know you have a lot on your plate, but we are hoping to set a date for his trial. -

-When? -

-Hopefully within the next two months. -

-I want to be there. -

-I figured that. I have some time on my hands until then. Want to go through your apartment. -

-Sure thing. I need to start clearing it out anyway. I'll get the cabin key from Jethro. -

-Alright. Just let me know. -

-I will. Keep me updated on your progress. -

Jethro came over and peeked over my shoulder at the conversation. He smiles and walks over to his key ring and puts the cabin key on my key ring. I smiled and sipped my tea, wanting the hot liquid to ease the pain. Jethro turned on the TV and once again the news blares nothing but Malachi. I don't want to see his face right now or even hear anything about him. Sensing my mood change, Jethro put an arm around me.

"Want me to find a movie or a show?"

I nod my head and he's switching the TV to his Netflix account. We watched three episodes of *The Witcher* before Jethro had an unexpected conference call. I was watching *Castle* when Julia walked in and I motioned for her to be silent as I nodded towards Jethro. Looking up and seeing her, though, he grabbed his computer and walked into the bedroom. Julia sat down as I grabbed my phone.

"Everything okay?"

-Conference call. -

"Oh."

-There's an ultimate fight in New York. One of them is a new fighter to the ring trying to make his name and wants Jethro to train him for the fight in his gym in New York. -

"That's great, right?"

-Yeah. -

I lowered my head after gazing toward our bedroom. Julia knew that look, so no words were necessary.

Ch. 28

Day one of the trial....

The courthouse was packed. The parking lot, the halls, and every inch of the courtroom. It wasn't even eight-thirty in the morning yet. As we pulled up, the media crowd out front made me shiver. I'm glad Julia told Jethro to park on the side. Malachi would be brought in through the front, through the crowds. I was a bundle of nerves, unsure about seeing him again. We waited three hours before Julia was calling to tell us it was time to come in. She was using me to try and get Malachi off guard. Outside the courtroom doors, we hear the judge.

"Malachi Peterson, you are on trial today for the murders of an astonishing one hundred and forty-four people. Your lawyer has you plead as not guilty. However, the FBI has a full confession from you. Your lawyer says you were under emotional distress. Anything changed that needs to be stated for the record before attorneys have their fun?"

That's when we hear D.A.'s voice break through the silence.

"Actually, your honor, we do. That count is not correct. It's only one hundred and forty-three. We have a survivor."

The doors open and Julia led us to our seats. The number of gaps we heard was like a gust of wind. I catch Malachi's stare. The surprise and guilt was evident on his face. The judge spoke to me before we slipped into our seats.

"Dr. Kniles, we are all so thankful that you are still with us and are terribly sorry for the ordeal you have been through."

I nod in acceptance as Jethro helps me sit down. The next two hours, I sat and listened to his lawyer and the defense attorney battle each other. The twelve jurors just listened as the rest of us did. Every once in a while, I feel Malachi's eyes on me as he looks back at us. Jethro puts a protective arm around me as he can tell Malachi is trying to get inside my head and Malachi's face turns red. Just like the rest of the viewers, I feel more and more sick as the pictures flash across the screen. The ones before he found me, those victims looked like they didn't suffer. The victims after, they suffered. Painfully. When they showed Elliot, I trembled and tried not to cry. Jethro grips my hand and whispered in my ear.

"Do you want to go?"

I shook my head and took a deep breath. I had to see this. How could I ever have thought I could change him? It was obvious that everyone in the room was affected as well. He was brutal, merciless, heartless. As I stared, that become more and more evident. He didn't do anything of this out of love. The rage that consumed his demon was all that mattered to him. Father was right. A demon could never feel love or even show it. He wasn't capable of it. How could I have been so blind before? I was now glad I had Jethro and gripped his hand tighter as the rest of the courtroom came to the same conclusion as me: Malachi couldn't be saved.

Ch. 29

Sleep didn't come that night. No matter how hard I tried, my mind wouldn't shut off. Malachi tried even harder to get into my head. There was a faint pressure at my temples. It was obvious by now to him that Michael had replaced his mark. He could no longer reach me. I got up and headed to the kitchen for a drink. I grabbed a bottle of water from the fridge and looked at the clock. It was 4:30 a.m. Jethro was still fast asleep. I could still hear his soft snoring. Me getting up hadn't disturbed his slumber. I found myself restless. I knew I wouldn't be able to get back to sleep no matter how hard I tried. I quickly penned a note to Jethro as I finish off the bottle.

Couldn't sleep. Went to my apartment to see what needs to be done. I love you.

I threw on some clothes, stuffed my keys into my pocket, and went to hail a cab. After getting dropped off, I scanned the sidewalk, just in case. I locked the door behind me and took a long look around. Some stuff had already been packed. Mainly, the big bulky stuff. Most kitchen appliances were in storage, everything in my living room was gone except for the couch. Really, all that was left was my patient papers and binders from the office, pictures, books. Small stuff like that. I scooted a tote box over to the bookshelf and started sorting through it. This box would be going to the cabin with me. I laid all my personal books at the bottom before sorting through files. Next, the pictures, folders, binders, and any other paper items went in. By the time the bookshelves were empty, it was close to seven a.m. Jethro would be waking up soon to open the gym by eight thirty. I grabbed a bottle of water out of my fridge and sank into the couch for just a moment. A quick peek at my phone revealed no texts or missed calls. What a relief.

I'm not sure when I had fallen asleep, but I was jolted awake by a pounding on my door. I rubbed sleep from my eyes before checking my phone. Not only was it close to ten a.m., but dozens of missed calls from Julia and even more so from Jethro. Then, there was all the texts from both of them asking where I was and if I was safe. What in the world was going on? The pounding at my door continued and I slowly walked to it. Looking through the peep hole, I saw Jethro standing on the other side. I unlocked it and he came rushing in. He didn't even stop to look at me before checking the whole apartment. When he was satisfied I was alone, he wrapped me in a hug and I felt him tremble.

"Malachi escaped this morning."

I felt my eyes grow wide and I knew I had gone pale. I wasn't expecting that.

"Julia came over as soon as she found out. I didn't see your note until I was grabbing my keys. I thought he..."

I hugged him this time. He thought Malachi had gotten me. When he let go, I walked over to the box by the bookshelf. He laughed when he saw and nodded his head. He called Julia and told her I was alright and that I had been packing. She hugged me when she got there and Jethro and Julia helped me pack the rest of the apartment. When nothing was left, Jethro went to get a moving truck. While he was gone, Julia got a call and slipped to the back room. I assumed it was from her bosses. I stood wondering if Jethro would want to keep my couch or sell it. There was a knock at the door and I assumed it was Jethro coming back. I wished I had looked before opening it. I panicked and tried to slam the door shut but Malachi stuck his foot out. I couldn't yell still, so I couldn't let Julia know. My phone was on the counter in the kitchen but I didn't dare turn my back on him again. Time stood still and I could see the venomous look in his eyes as he glared at me. Remembering the last time I saw him, I reached for my neck. He noticed the movement and I saw guilt flood his face. I reached out to Michael.

Michael! Malachi's here! Julia is on the phone. Michael, please!

I'm on the elevator, baby, just hang on!

Michael!

I'm here!

Before Malachi could blink, Michael threw himself on him and they both tumbled to the ground inside the apartment. The noise brought Julia out and while she was still on the phone told all units to converge on her location. She tried to get Jethro off of him, but he wasn't Jethro at the moment. He was Michael the archangel and he was beating Malachi to death as only Michael can. Other agents got there and managed to pull him off and get Malachi out. Michael wrapped an arm around me protectively as Malachi glared at him. Michael had won. Not just my heart, but the fight for me and Malachi knew he couldn't best him. He had lost me.

Ch.30

I was now confined to the cabin. It had been too close of a call last time and Jethro wasn't taking any chances. Malachi's guilt was the only thing that bought Jethro enough time to get there. As if things couldn't get worse, the stupid judge gave him a death sentence. He can't die. He'll fake it long enough and then come right back for me.

Jethro was packing up his condo since my apartment had been finished and listed. I had boxes everywhere that still needed to be unpacked. My favorite in the cabin was now my claw-footed tub that Jethro surprised me with. I had my voice back. I could talk, but yelling was still out of the question. I felt cramped inside the cabin and went for a walk to the water's edge. I remember what Father had said and closed my eyes, envisioning my wings. A euphoric feeling overtook me and I opened my eyes. I couldn't help the smile that spread across my face. Silver tipped white wings expanded on either side of my back. I was lost in admiration that I didn't hear Jethro walk up.

"You got your wings back!?"

I jumped and my wings folded into me.

"I didn't mean to scare you."

"It's okay. I just didn't hear you."

"Your wings?"

"You've got yours, too."

He took a step back and imagined it. Solid black wings expanded on either side of him and burst into laughter. He wrapped me in a hug and his wings engulfed me, making me feel safe and warm.

"When did you know?"

"When I was in a coma this time."

"What!? You knew this whole time?"

"I did tell you there were things we had to talk about."

"Speaking of which..."

"I know. You want to know what happened."

"I think I need to."

"You do."

I took a deep breath and sat on the rocky shore.

"It all happened in flashes at first. Just scenes from a movie while I was still in a coma."

"You knew before you were discharged and you didn't tell me?"

"I didn't know if you were you or Michael. Plus, I didn't really understand it."

"But you still called to me."

"Yes. After I got back to the condo, the images got worse. I decided I needed answers and I felt like Malachi was the only one who could give me those answers. That's when I went to go find him. I ended up finding him at the docks."

"The docks!?"

"I know. But, Michael, when I saw him and he saw me, it was like the fourth of July fireworks. It was indescribable."

"If it was so good, why call me?"

"After we got to the hotel, even before, it felt wrong. I wanted you. He could tell. I told him I wanted you. When I turned to leave, he snapped. In that moment, I just hoped you could hear me."

"Serenity, I..."

"I love you, Michael. It was you. I chose you and Father gave us our wings back. He did give me a choice to stay here or return with him. I chose to stay. He said you are free to make your own choice now that your wings are back."

"Serenity, anywhere you are is where I want to be. If here is where you wish to stay, then I'll be right here with you. I shouldn't have gotten so angry at you. I'm sorry. I wish you had told me sooner, though."

"I know. But we can put this behind us, though, right?"

"Of course. What do we do when he gets out?"

"I want to tell Julia. She can his sentence changed."

"If that's what you want to do, then I support you. I still have to fly to New York to help train this kid. Have her stay here with you."

"Jethro..."

"This is something you need to be alone with her."

He was right. I just hoped I didn't freak her out too bad. Jethro kissed the top of my head before disappearing back up the beach. I knew things would be different now. I wanted us to be happy. I just wondered how long it would last now that the archangel had his wings back.

Ch.31

Jethro had been gone three days now. Julia agreed to stay with me at the cabin. We were currently sitting on the couch watching a movie. Once it was over, I switched off the TV and she turned to me.

"Everything okay?"

"We need to talk."

"Okay?"

"Let's take a walk. To the beach."

She nodded and followed me out the door. I decided not to beat around the bush. Not with Julia. We walked along the rocky shore, not saying a word. She was waiting for me.

"So, do you remember all those years ago when Jethro made the ridiculous notion that we were fallen angels and that's why we are the way we are?"

"Of course. He was kind of obsessed about it."

"Right and you said there was no way it could be true."

"Yeah."

"What if it was?"

"Serena...."

"Let me finish, please."

Julia nodded her head and I tried to think of the best way to tell her.

"I thought it was absurd, too. Then, the accident happened. I was shown things. Memories from a previous life where my name was Serenity. I had silver tipped white wings. Jethro is actually the archangel, Michael. There was war. Demons and angels fighting alongside humans. I myself was almost killed. I was whisked away and tainted and fell in love with a demon name Malachi. He forever put his mark on me and I was punished. My wings were stripped. Michael kept watch over my imprisonment after my wounds had killed me. This life is my second chance. Jethro or Malachi? After I realized all this, I went searching for Malachi. I needed answers that only he could give me. I was stupid in thinking things would be the same. Not only was he worse, but I changed. I only wanted Michael. I tried to leave Malachi and when he tried to kill me, I reached out to Michael. After I had woken up, Malachi could still reach me because of the mark he put on me. He could still play with my mind. At court that day, he realized he couldn't reach me anymore which meant Michael had put his mark on me forever blocking him from reaching my mind ever again. It enraged him. That's why he escaped. Malachi can't be killed, Julia. When he gets injected, he'll stop his heart long enough to be pronounced dead. When they carry him out, he'll just come back for me. I can prove all of this."

"Selena, I just..."

I stopped her mid-sentence when I spread my wings and she stood in awe. She hesitantly reached out and touched them.

"They're so soft."

"Do you believe me, now?"

"Kind of hard not to."

"Julia, I need you to stop his death sentence."

"I'll do what I can. I promise."

She pulled me in for a hug and whispered that she loved me. I said it back as my wings wrapped around her and she giggled. I felt a lot better now that she knew everything. I was confident Julia would work her magic and get his sentence changed.

Ch.32

As expected, Jethro and I fought constantly. With his wings back, he didn't want to stay and tried to convince me otherwise. That or threatened to leave time and time again. I loved being in Seattle, though. I got mad and told him he could do whatever he wanted to do. I didn't really need him. That was a lie, of course. I loved him and couldn't stand the thought of losing him.

I sat on the treetops a good distance away from everything. I could feel Michael trying to reach out, but I blocked him out. The spot I picked was far from view, so it would take some time to find me if he tried looking for me. I watched the sun set and the birds play in and out of the clouds. I felt him before I heard him. He landed and his wings settled behind me. He wrapped his arms around me and pulled me close to him.

"I'm sorry. I know this place is important to you."

"I chose not to go with Father because of the life we built here."

"I understand that now."

"My clients are thrilled I'm back in the office."

"I know. I honestly wasn't thinking about all of that."

I looked back at him and saw him taking in the view before us.

"You picked quite the spot to hide from me."

I smiled before leaning my head against his chest. A peaceful silence fell over us as we just sat and enjoyed each other's company. We must've sat about two hours before I heard my phone ring. It was Julia.

"Hey, I'm at the cabin. Where are you two?"

"Jethro and I got into it and I had to leave for a bit."

"Oh? Should I come back?"

"No. It's all good. We worked it out."

"Okay."

"Be down in a second."

Julia watched as our feet hit the ground. Our wings folded behind us as she smiled and shook her head.

"I don't think I'll ever get used to that."

I laughed and hugged her. We went to the back porch and sat on the chairs. Jethro walked inside.

"What's going on?"

"Well, I have some good news for you."

"Oh?"

"After a long back and forth debate with the DA and the judge, I got him resentenced."

"To what?"

"He is now looking at ten years per person."

"Oh wow, that's...."

"Right now, it's forty-seven and half life sentences."

"Holy crap."

"It gets better. While you were in a coma, he admitted to a few murders in Canda so their government tacked on another forty years."

"So, he's not getting out?"

"No. Not on good behavior or parole."

"Thank you so much, Jules."

"Of course. You may be an angel, but it's still my job to protect you."

I hugged her as Jethro came out.

"Did you hear?"

"How could I not? Your thoughts were so loud."

"You can hear her thoughts?"

"Yes, but just hers because of the mark."

Julia simply nodded her head. All of this was still pretty new to her and she was trying to understand it all. I was a bit upset, however. With the case officially over, Julia would be moving to Virginia. I followed her inside as she got up to leave. I handed her a note for Malachi. She read it and laughed. Sort of my icing on the cake to him. Jethro found it amusing when I showed it to him when I first wrote it. After Julia left, he wrapped me in a hug and kissed my neck.

"Anything you'd like to do tonight?"

"Space Needle for dinner?"

"Perfect. I'll make reservations."

I kissed him before walking into our bathroom. I planned on soaking until I absolutely had to get out. I laid there, soaking with my eyes closed. I felt Jethro's gaze and peeked up at him. He just smiled at me.

"What?"

"You are just so beautiful when you are that relaxed."

He winked at me before claiming my lips. As he walked out, he looked over his shoulder.

"Reservations are at eight. It's six-thirty now."

I smiled as I soaked deeper into the water. Things couldn't possibly get any better than this.

Ch.33

I was probably the happiest inmate on death row. The stupid humans didn't know I can't die. It would be a matter of time before I got my angel back. I laughed just thinking about it and it caused the inmates beside me to call me a mad man. I guess I was in a way. I had been here six weeks already. When the warden walked up with a handful of guards, I smiled thinking it was time.

"What's going on? Is it time, already?"

"You don't get that lucky, Malachi. Judge resentenced you."

"What!?"

"Forty-eight life sentences."

"That's ridiculous!"

"Special Agent Kniles will be here in the next few days to speak with you."

They shut my cell door and I was left seething on my bunk. Who in the world has that kind of sentence? It was an outrage. Special Agent Kniles and I would have words indeed. I needed to see Serenity.

Two days after I got moved to lockdown and solitary confinement, Julia showed up. I got put into a small room and shackled to the table and floor. She sat down and took a small piece of paper out of her coat pocket. I knew it was from Serenity.

"I want to know what she said."

"And you will."

"Does she know?"

"Who do you think convinced me to get you resentenced?"

"Liar! She wouldn't!"

"You almost killed her. What makes you different to her than Elliott?"

"No! I'm nothing like him!"

"You're right. You're worse."

"What did she say?"

Julia stared at me for a moment and I was afraid she wouldn't give me the note. Eventually, she unfolded the paper and slid it to me.

Malachi,

By now I know you've guessed that Michael has replaced your mark. I will never see you again and I'm happy about that. I'm happy with Michael. You hurt me, Malachi, worse than Elliott ever did. By choosing Michael, Father gave us our wings back. Showing Julia was how I convinced her to get you resentenced. She knows exactly who and what you are as well. I hope you've realized by now with our wings back, we'll be going back to Father. This is also the last time you will see Julia. I truly hope you rot in there before returning to Hell. Good-bye, Malachi.

Serenity

I couldn't help but stare at it as I read it over and over again. I looked up at Julia.

"This can't be true?"

"It is. I said farewell yesterday."

"She's really gone?"

"Her and Michael both."

"NO!"

"They are where they belong and so are you."

"No..."

"You're right, but you'll get there. I wonder what the punishment for failing in pursuit of love is? I can't imagine it's good."

"No, but I deserve it if I've truly lost her."

"Good-bye, Malachi."

She got up to leave, but I had to know one more thing before she left.

"Was she happy?"

"The happiest I've seen her."

I just nodded my head as the guard opened the door and ushered her out. They came in, got me, and led me back to my cell. Serenity was gone. I had lost my angel. There was really nothing left for me here anymore. It was time for me to return home, no matter what that meant for me.

Ch.34

Three years later......

I sat at the hotel bar sipping the glass of whiskey in front of me. I wore a skin-tight black cocktail dress. I was bait for a new case. A new target. His victims: beautiful and wealthy looking women. I listened into everyone's thoughts around me as I waited to hear his. I could feel eyes on me from across the room and I focused a bit more.

Look at this entitled bitch. Sitting there like she thinks she owns the room. Bitch probably thinks she can have any man with a snap of her fingers. I'll snap something for you alright, bitch.

I reached out to Jethro, who sat in a van outside with Julia.

He's taken the bait.

Alright. We're ready. Jeremy is positioned upstairs. Be careful.

Our connection was broken when someone touched my elbow. I turned to look at a man with dark skin, dark hair, and brown eyes. He was handsome but his eyes held a certain ruthlessness that made me shiver.

"Forgive me, but I couldn't help but notice you are drinking alone."

"And if I am?"

"By choice?"

"I'm celebrating my divorce."

"Oh, I'm sorry."

"I'm not. He was an unfaithful bastard."

"Mind if I join you, then? A woman so beautiful should never have to drink alone."

"Sure. I'd love some charming company."

"If it's charming you want, why don't we get a room?"

"I have a room."

He smiled as I let him help me from the barstool. I led to the elevators and we rode up to the fifth-floor suites. I was nervous the whole way. They had to catch him in the act. Jethro didn't like it because I'd have to be put in harm's way.

Once in the room, he eyed me like a predator eyes its prey. I took a deep breath as I turned my back on him, knowing he would strike. He didn't disappoint. I fell forward and he flipped me over. He dragged me by the ankle as I tried to crawl away, screaming for help.

"Shut up, bitch! You think your self-entitled attitude is going to save you? Bitch, I'll show you!"

He climbed on top of me and his hands wrapped around my throat. That's when Jeremy burst into the room from the bathroom. He ripped the guy off of me as Julia and her team came in.

"Dennis Warwick! You are under arrest for the murder of six women."

An agent hauled him up, cuffed him, and read him his rights. Jethro came in after he was gone and raised an eyebrow at me. He hadn't seen the dress yet.

"The things I could do to you right now, woman."

"Home isn't that far, Jet."

"We won't make it."

He gave Julia a dark look as he shut the hotel door. I laughed as I heard her in the hallway.

"Dr. Kniles has clean up."

Two years ago, the FBI offered me a job as the department's psychologist. Listening to their thoughts was a minefield of its own. They saw and heard things that normal people didn't. After I got the job, Jethro opened a new gym out here and the FBI got a discount. It all happened by accident, too. Jethro was out here for a fight and some agents went. Afterwards, I heard one of the agents considering suicide and gave him my card. Two months after that, the FBI offered me the job. Jethro, of course, hated moving to a more crowded area, but he knew how much I missed Julia. The year apart was misery. After we moved, he proposed. I said yes, obviously. He was worrying me, though, as he seemed so bored with our lives. I mean, our lives were busy and we argued a bit, but something else was wrong. I prayed to Father for guidance on what to do. I want to understand how to help him. I'd do anything to make Michael happy, short of actually going home.

Ch. 35

Two years had gone by since I prayed for guidance about Michael. How was this the answer? I sat in the doctor's office and stared at the tiny figure on the screen. I went a bit numb hearing its tiny heartbeat. The sonographer printed out the pictures and I was headed home. Jethro and I never talked about kids. Mostly because we didn't think it was possible. I pulled up into our driveway and was relieved to find Jethro's car gone. Once inside, I called Julia.

"Special Agents Kniles."

"Jules."

"Selena? What's wrong? You okay?"

"Can you come over?"

"I'm on my way."

Twenty minutes later, Julia knocked on the door. Before she could hammer me with questions, I showed her the pictures and sat down on the couch. She was stunned to silence as she sat down beside me on the couch.

"I didn't think...."

"Me too."

"Jethro?"

"Doesn't know yet."

"So?"

"We never talked about...."

"You're scared he might leave?"

"Maybe. You've seen him lately. He's just so bored and unhappy."

I took the pictures back and placed them back inside my bag.

"I think you need to just tell him."

"Tell me what?"

We both jumped at the sound of Jethro's voice.

"What's going on?"

"I'll leave you to it. If it does go south, you can always come stay with me."

Jethro came around to me, now more worried than ever.

"What is it?"

Just like with Julia, I didn't say a word as I handed him the pictures. He stared in disbelief and wonderment. His eyes met mine in a sincere look and

I waited on baited breath for him to say something. He smiled as he wrapped his arms around my waist and said a small thank you to Father. Now, I was confused. I'm glad my face showed it because I don't think I could have said a word at that moment.

"You've been watching families here lately and I asked Father that if having a family of your own was something your heart desired, maybe he could bless us. So, he has."

I felt the tear well up in my eyes as I tried to speak.

"You...you did this...for me?"

"Of course. I would do anything to make you happy."

I felt ashamed and let him listen to my thoughts. I felt guilty that I thought he may leave because he seemed so unsatisfied and all the while, he was trying to make me happy. I called Julia and let her know and she was overjoyed, saying she knew Jethro would never leave. She did tell me, however, that since I was expecting, I would be confined to the office. This made Jethro stress a lot less about me working. I felt the excitement at the thought of having my own family and couldn't keep the smile off my face as Jethro rubbed my stomach.

There was a knock on my office door a few months later. An agent that had a file for me to look at Julia's request. By now, I looked like I swallowed a whole watermelon and didn't really get out of my office unless I had to. I stared in confusion at the blank document before.

"This is blank?"

"I don't know, Dr. Kniles. Special Agent Kniles said if there was any problems, to go see her."

I groaned. She knew I had problems getting up and down. I walked out as the entire office said surprise in unison. It was a going away party. This was my last day as the baby was due in three weeks. She didn't disappoint, our little angel. Sienna Grace Knight made her appearance into the world with wisps of red and blonde hair and deep brown eyes. Julia thought she was precious but got upset because Jethro refused to share her.

After I recovered, Jethro and I got married and have been married for four months now. I was Dr. Knight at work and Mrs. Knight everywhere else. Jethro and I were more content that we had been in a while and I knew this perfect little angel sitting on my chest was the reason for that.

Back at work, Jeremy paid me a visit.

"Hey, Doc, you got a second?"

"Of course."

He walked in and set a file on my desk. Inside were pictures of Malachi's cell. Everything inside was charred. I smiled as I closed the folder. The demon had returned to Hell.

Epilogue

Ten years later......

    I stood on the balcony of our beach front home. The sun was warm, the birds were laughing, and below me on the beach ran part of my whole world. Jethro was chasing ten-year old Sienna, eight-year-old Ryan, and six-year-old Blake down the sand dunes. Their laughter was carried on the wind to my spot. I couldn't help but smile. Behind me, laying in their bed, two-year old twins, Mariah and Mandy were taking an afternoon nap. As I saw Jethro wave up to me, I rubbed circles on my growing middle. Jethro and I have been married for nine years now and have five children with one on the way. Life in general seemed brighter after the day I found out Malachi had gone back to Hell. I knew he couldn't hurt me or my children. Feeling this happiness when surrounded by my family, I understood how humans questioned whether Heaven was better or not.

    I closed my eyes and felt the salty breeze as I looked back on everything that had gotten me to this point. Honestly, I would have laughed if someone told me that this is what my future looked like. After losing mom and dad, the stuff with Elliot, and then, of course, Malachi, life just seemed so dark. Julia had been a light for me, but no one shined brighter in my darkness than Jethro. After Malachi literally killed me, Jethro was all I knew I would ever need. As strange and horrific as it was, I wouldn't change any of it. I wouldn't be where I am right now if I had. It brought Jethro and I so much closer than before. Redeemed not only my wings, but his as well. Now, Father tells me, when all the kids get old enough, they too shall have wings and abilities. Jethro and I never hide who we are to the kids so they may understand one day. I just pray they don't make the same mistakes I did in life. I hope they always follow their hearts and choose the right path, as it will be the path that leads back to Father. It took me thirty-two years to get where I am now. Of course, not counting the centuries I remained lost in some sleep while Michael guarded over me. My other prayer was that they find someone who will love them and never give up on them as Michael does with me. Michael gave up everything, even as an archangel, to help me redeem myself. His loyalty and love for me knows no bounds.

Inside, having heard all my thoughts, Jethro settled the kids in the living room before kissing me on that balcony. I silently thanked Father for His forgiveness, but also Michael's love. As I looked at my little family with Jethro, I smiled. Turned out, a wingless love here on earth was exactly what I needed. I never dreamed of having any of this for myself. Not only was I forgiven, but I was with the man I was destined to be with and life simply flourished with him. Michael and Serenity; a love designed by God Himself.